DREAMING *of* PALESTINE

DREAMING
_of_ PALESTINE

A Novel of Friendship, Love & War by

RANDA GHAZY

Translated from the Italian by

MARGUERITE SHORE

GEORGE BRAZILLER PUBLISHER

New York

Originally published in Italy under the title *Sognando Palestina* by RCS Libri
S.p.A. Milano–Fabbri in 2002.

First published in the United States of America in 2003
by George Braziller, Inc.

For information, please address the publisher:
George Braziller, Inc.
171 Madison Avenue
New York, NY 10016

Library of Congress Cataloging-in-Publication Data

Ghazy, Randa
    [Sognando Palestina. English]
    Dreaming of Palestine / Randa Ghazy ; translated from the Italian by
    Marguerite Shore.
       p. cm.
    ISBN 0-8076-1522-6
    I. Shore, Marguerite. II. Title.

    PQ4907.H39S6413 2003
    853'.92—dc21   2003050302

Design by Rita Lascaro
Printed and bound in the United States of America
FIRST EDITION

There are many, too many, people I would like to thank.
For this reason I will limit myself to mentioning
the most important: Davide, he knows why;
Marina, who has dreamed with me;
my parents, because what I am and say and write
is the result of what they have done;
my father, because he is the one who
made me understand that the Palestinians are our
brothers and that their suffering must come to an end;
Beatrice and Cristina, who made it possible
for me to accomplish my life dream;
and above all my sister Rasha,
who has been with me in every hard-earned line of this book
and who has had the enormous
patience to stay by my side, always.
Thank you.

I shall resist without fear. Yes, without fear, I shall resist.
On my country's land, I shall resist.
Whoever steals from me all that I have, I shall resist.
Whoever murders my children, I shall resist.
Whoever blows up my house,
O, my beloved house!
In the shadow of your walls, I shall resist.

I shall resist without fear...

With all the strength of my soul, I shall resist.
With my staff, with my knife, I shall resist.
Flag in hand, I shall resist.
If they cut off my hand
and soil my flag,
with my other hand, I shall resist.

I shall resist without fear...

Inch by inch, in my field, in my garden, I shall resist.
With faith and will, I shall resist.
With my nails and with my teeth, I shall resist.
And when even my body
is nothing more than a gash,
with the blood of my wounds, I shall resist.
I shall resist without fear...

— ANONYMOUS PALESTINIAN

PART ONE

"WHY AM I ALWAYS THE ONE? HUH? ISN'T THERE ANYONE else who can take my place? Hey, what the devil, there's Ramy! Make him do it! I'm fed up! There's no way I'm your servant! What the hell, do you think I look like a servant? Gihad, according to you, do I look like a servant? Tell the truth now! A servant?"

"No, you don't look like a servant, Ibrahim! Not at all, on the contrary, you look like an emperor! A Greek emperor who . . . "

"Cut out the bullshit, Gihad! And what sort of name is that, anyway, that you have? What kind of name is Gihad?"

"Gihad is a glorious name! You know, it's one of those names that was conned . . . canned . . . candid . . . "

"Coined! Names coined in times of war! You've told us this story two thousand times!"

"That's it, thanks, Nedal, and don't tell us that your name, too, was coined . . . canned . . . conned . . . "

"Coined!"

"That's it, coined in times of war! It means a courageous man, who doesn't give up, who fights? Because we . . . "

"Be quiet, Gihad! In fact, why don't *you* go? No way am I

[11]

a servant! Why do I always have to do it? Do I maybe look like a servant? Ahmed, according to you, do I look like a servant?"

"Huh? What did you say, Ibrahim?"

"Put down that damned book, Ahmed, and tell me: do I look like a servant?"

"Look, it's a wonderful book . . . did you know that smokers are less likely than nonsmokers to come down with Alzheimer's disease?"

"Come on, Ahmed, put down that damned book and tell me: do I look like a servant?"

"I don't understand why you say it in such a disparaging tone! Since time immemorial, servants have toiled away with tremendous courage! They have worked, sweated, muscles trained, with such strength in their arms, impassive, without showing a hint of exasperation or loss of dignity . . . "

"What the hell does that have to do with anything? Ahmed, I just asked you: do I look like a servant?"

"I wouldn't know, I think that . . . hey, Ualid, you're back! How long does it take to buy a pack of cigarettes, anyway? We have a tobacconist at the corner, the market across the street . . . "

"You say across the street, but it's six hundred meters from here!"

"So? You're young, you should be in good enough shape to run! And hey, these are Philip Morris! I asked you for Marlboro Light! Don't you even know how to buy a pack of cigarettes? Fifteen years old and he doesn't know how to go buy a pack of cigarettes? Can you explain what's going on in your head? What's that you're holding?"

BAM!

"Dear God, what's going on? Not even my mother has

slapped me around like this! What's bugging you, Ahmed? I didn't do anything!"

"Since when do you smoke, you jerk? Drop that cigarette right away! No, give it to me, here!...Aaah...you know, I haven't had a smoke for two days? And this is the last time, you dope, if you want to hang out with us, you can't be seen again with a cigarette in your hand!"

"But you're all smoking!"

"You're only fifteen, idiot!"

"But Mohammad and Ramy have been smoking since they were twelve!"

"That's their business! What an imbecile you are! You know, how is it that you're hanging out with us? Why have we taken you on? No, explain it to me, please, because I have completely forgotten...how is it that we were so stupid to let you hang out with us? Huh?"

"I'm sorry, I'm sorry, Ahmed, I promise that it won't happen again, really! I'm sorry! Ibrahim, you tell him!"

"Come on, Ahmed, Ualid is right! He won't do it any more, come on...listen, Ualid: according to you, do I look like a servant? No, tell me the truth, tell me, do I have a face like a servant?"

"Like a servant? Well, I don't know...no, I don't think you, well maybe a bit, you know, you have bushy eyebrows and your forehead is too high and your complexion is like dirty coffee, and then you always have dirty ears and big nostrils..."

"But how dare you? Look this...dirty coffee? Well, look at you, what a lowlife!"

BAM!

"Ow! What have you done now? Ouch, it hurts...is everyone hitting me today? Go bugger..."

BAM!

"There, good, run away, or I'd hit you again a third time, otherwise . . . look at these young people, rude beyond belief . . . did you see, Ahmed?"

"Well, I don't know what to say, maybe we were a little tough . . . "

"Stop being a wimp! He is the youngest, our hopes rest on him! And he is our future, don't you understand? We have to back him up, always, no matter what! Mothers come in handy for slaps and cuddles, but we, instead, are only for slaps! Understand, we have to educate him, but we also have to help him become tough, otherwise we'll find ourselves with a fairy who faints at the sight of blood!"

"I don't know, maybe you're right . . . "

"Listen, getting back to our earlier conversation, do you think I look like a servant? No, really, because, sorry, it's not right that I'm the one who always has to go to the well. And, we've had no water for a week now! What the devil is going on? So, do I look like a servant?"

"I wouldn't know, Ibrahim, it's just that you don't really have a refined face . . . "

"And what does that have to do with it? Listen a moment, I am Ibrahim Samir Sayed al Ramadan! Does that seem like nothing to you? Huh? Maybe I look like a servant?"

"I don't know, I wouldn't know . . . Ibrahim looks like a servant?"

"For God's sake, shut up already, Gihad! Do you want this or not? God almighty . . . will you stop it? Get off it, stop! Get out of here! Well, what do you say, Ahmed? Like a servant? I wouldn't know. In Egypt I have a friend who resembles him, but he's a guy who has a pile of money, and an upper-crust family to back him up, rich for generations."

"There, you see, Ahmed? Look at these idiotic fools. Thanks, Riham! You're wonderful! And now get going to the well, idiot. Will you look at these fools..."

"What do you mean? I'm not going to be the one who goes to the well! What if I meet up with a soldier? And I end up with a bullet in my head? Wouldn't you kill yourself then, out of remorse, out of guilt? God, what cruelty! And if they surround me? And if they kill me? Do you want me to die like that, alone like a dog? Because of you, then...?"

"Ok, calm down, there's no reason to make a fuss! Ualid! Ualid!"

"Yes, what is it?"

"Take the bucket and go get some water."

"Me? But I just went to buy cigarettes!"

"I don't give a damn, go, before you get another slap!"

"Ok...damn."

"Are you happy, you idiot? Now if the soldiers have to kill someone, it will be a young boy of fifteen!"

"Oh, for God's sake, don't make me feel guilty. And if the soldiers really get him? Well, you know...listen, take my book and put it in your backpack. I'm going with Ualid, I'll be right back..."

"God, what a dope. You actually have to talk about death to get him moving. Look at these youngsters..."

Ibrahim glances over at Ahmed's book, which isn't teaching him anything, anyway—nothing. He has never liked books. He doesn't understand why they always forced him to read; it was something he hated, just hated. It bored him to death; he preferred playing soccer with his friends. Meanwhile, Ahmed, who always ended up as goalie since he was the player who mattered least, could even read on the toilet, or even while he was playing, as goalie, between shots, though it must be said that in the end he didn't block a single goal, not one. He never showed any ability, but he still had to play goalie. And no one else ever wanted that position, because they all wanted to be the top scorers, they wanted to be heroes, always, in everything . . .

The only book Ibrahim reads willingly is the Qur'an. It is a passion handed down from his father, who was a muezzin in the largest and most popular mosque in the city. He was a very religious man, a great man, killed by the war—he too— only it wasn't reported on television. After all, it hardly matters if the world gets to know about him, since the world doesn't give a damn—not a damn—if one more dies, or one less. These are only numbers, understand, only numbers, and they limit themselves to saying "what a shame," or maybe not even anything, because they are too busy flipping channels. But in the end it hardly matters, who cares, it isn't their battle, it's not theirs, it is the Palestinians' battle, that's all, and it has nothing to do with the part of the world that watches television. Certainly not. Even if some minister of foreign affairs in some country or other speaks with the leaders of the two sides. Even if the American president organizes a meeting, even if the UN secretary-general issues confident and concerned statements, it's not about them, and they know it full well, because they are the ones— they—who have kept their distance. We know that absolutely nothing matters to them, nothing; they are busy with other events, and this, they, the Palestinians, they know it, know it well, and maybe among them, might you find an Egyptian, or a Syrian, or a Jordanian? But don't you find it sad that it hardly matters, because there will only be two or three, and in the end the Palestinians know they are alone? That's how it is, really—we all know it—we are all waiting to lose, we believe that we'll lose, doesn't that seem easier to you? The head of the PLO is assassinated, Mama America rebukes Israel (yeah, right), the world watches, the Palestinians respond. Mama America calls them terrorists (really?), the world watches, it's obvious that the Israelis aren't terrorists—nooooo—they're only poor soldiers with some little machine guns and a few tanks. Instead, look at the Palestinians, what assassins, with those advanced weapons, those oh-so-sophisticated and modern devices—are those stones?—those powerful and well-aimed rocks, with their superorganized military forces, the world watches. Ibrahim drinks a glass of water. Ualid and Ahmed come back. No soldier has killed them, and once again fear has been defeated, but what a fright, anyway. The Italian minister of foreign affairs has spoken to Arafat, but what will change? A sixty-year-old Israeli was killed in the West Bank; Sharon wants a seven-day truce. Ibrahim holds the photo of his father, he looks at it, his sharp features, his proud gaze, that light in his eyes. Mama America continues to send little gifts to the Israelis—little gifts, little gifts that kill, weapons—the world watches, a tear runs down Ibrahim's cheek. But no, no, he is a man, a man. They have always taught him this, to be a man, no tears, he must be strong, MUST BE, of necessity, for how can you fight a war crying? You can't, the world is watching, watching, the world is watching.

"Riham! Riham! Hurry up, for heaven's sake, what are you doing? Ah, well, ok, you're right...you're always fixing things to eat. I feel a bit sorry for you, maybe it's better to risk one's life, or at least to go out, come out from hiding, instead of staying in the house, preparing meals for everyone. What are we eating? Chickpeas again, good heavens, is that the only thing you know how to make?"

"Ibrahim, today we're having chickpeas with sauce, and listen, I know how to cook a bunch of other things, but as long as Ualid brings me only chickpeas from the market, what else can I cook?"

"Why does that idiot Ualid get only chickpeas?"

"Maybe because the money you give him isn't enough to get anything other than chickpeas? It's an interesting theory, think about it."

"What's this, you're making fun of me, woman?"

"The woman has a name, man."

"Don't be sarcastic."

"And you, don't be so rude."

"I really would like to know why Nedal married you."

"Because he's not like you, thank God! And now go call the others, since it's ready, and stop with those disgusting cigarettes that smoke up this hovel. I, who have never touched a cigarette, smell more than all of you, and my lungs are in shreds!"

The men sit at the table. Ualid brings in the bread. Riham puts three, four plates on the little table, and each soaks the bread in the sauce, taking chickpeas by the spoonful, eating in silence, each immersed in his own thoughts. Only Ualid continues to complain because he is crowded and squashed in between Mohammad, whose bulk is considerable, and Ibrahim, who doesn't sit properly when he eats and stretches out his arms and legs, at the expense of his neighbors. Then silence, only the noise of spoons and lips sucking up the sauce. Then Ibrahim speaks. He says that in the next village over, three boys died today. When two soldiers arrived, they heard some noises, turned around and shot. One of the soldiers was struck by a stone, his eye was hurt, nothing too serious. Nedal retorts that an Israeli soldier was stoned in

Rafah. Ramy chimes in about a woman and her husband, she was killed and he seriously wounded, in Hebron, by a group of Israeli soldiers. Then complete silence, they finish eating.

They get up slowly, each does something, each goes about his chores. Riham goes to wash the dishes and make tea, Nedal gets up to help her, and Ibrahim follows him to tell him something.

Ahmed has a pistol, he got it off a dead Israeli soldier, and he takes it out every day and polishes it, carefully, attentively. It seems so important to him. Once Ualid asked if he could touch it and Ahmed said no, that it was dangerous, and Ualid insisted, asking why it had to be dangerous. And at a certain point he touched it, he picked it up. Ahmed fell upon him, and bam, there was a punch, then a shout. Everyone ran into the room, and when they saw Ualid on the floor with his hands above his head, and Ahmed bent over him, trembling, they all burst out laughing. God, what a dope, what a dope, rather both of you, such idiots and cowards . . .

All together, like that, they give each other strength. They laugh at their own nonsense, they laugh, they must, that they should be serious in a situation like this; it's wartime, nothing more, there are people dying, lives shattered, destinies, lives, understand? Lives, but there is strength to laugh over something funny—there is—maybe to keep from crying, maybe because they want to convince themselves that there is something normal in their lives, because they want to reclaim the tranquillity of everyday things and domestic banalities. And that's why, they know it, they are grown men against the war, boys who play at being grownups because someone is forcing them to play grown-ups, who would like to be young, with the bodies and ideals of grown-ups but the feelings, weaknesses, fears of children.

The war has made them grow up, that's how it is. They didn't want it this way, but that's how it is, like that Gamal. Twenty years old, young, naive, he didn't even have a middle-school diploma, and he didn't even know who Kofi Annan was (that day he saw him on television he asked who he was), and yet sometimes he was there with them, smoking their cigarettes, praying with them, eating chickpeas with them, taking their advice and hurling insults at Sharon, dirty assassin, without in reality even knowing what his face looked like, what he had done in life—he only knew that he was a dirty assassin. That's how it was. Gamal had accepted a hatred that was not his own, it was that of an entire people, and he had done so in such a way that he shaped it within his own personality (which, moreover, wasn't terribly strong, he never spoke, ate little, smoked little, no excesses and no martyrs' ideals). There you have it, Gamal, with his tobacco spat out on the ground. His mother had been raped, and then she was killed by his father; his father had been put in jail, but he strangled himself with his inmate's T-shirt. His brothers, all younger, were parceled out along the way, his sister married a man who was never home. There you have it, this shattered family, this flat personality, these words—dirty assassin—spat out along with his Drum cigarettes, without really even knowing why, that's it, that's it and nothing more, there you have it. That's how Gamal grew up, badly, in a hurry, with no choice possible—no one had that—and everyone knew that it would happen. They all knew it, that's what it was like. He would do something, sooner or later, something. No one wanted it, no one, no, Gamal, no, why? There are other ways, but instead, like that, he approached an Israeli military base, they had to search him and then, at a certain point . . .

There, at a certain point the bomb exploded, his chest smashed into clumps, pieces, fragments of flesh, his body exploded, he alone blew up an entire Israeli checkpoint, five soldiers died along with him, five. In the wake of the hundreds all over the place, one might ask, why, finally, why throw away your life to kill only five enemies? It's an insignificant number, and your country needs you in other ways, why? But no one has an answer. A kiss, be careful, we'll miss you, you're brave, truly, I mean it seriously, I don't know if I could ever do it, we'll all always remember you, we will win, we will win, thanks to you as well, you who have God with you, and they had let him go—they had let him go—and after some twenty or so minutes, a few kilometers away, a bomb exploded, Gamal exploded, and a checkpoint and five soldiers—others were wounded, some survived—and on TV they didn't even mention him. They spoke about Arafat, who had to respond to Sharon, who wanted a seven-day truce, but that wasn't war—it wasn't—nor was it the truth. They should have spoken about Gamal, not Sharon—what is Sharon doing now, maybe drinking his tea at home—but it's always like this, always, we can't do anything about it. No one had known Gamal, no one knew about the Drum cigarettes he smoked and the words he spoke—dirty assassin— no one had ever known him.

But war is like that.

PART TWO

CERTAIN THINGS JUST HAPPEN, LIKE THAT. MAYBE PEOPLE make choices, and so the bizarre course of events, coincidences, come to pass and you find yourself in a certain phase of your life and you wonder: but how did I get here? And this was what Ibrahim was wondering, how had he gotten here, what had his life been before finding a goal and people with whom he could achieve it, people who thought like you, who shared your ideals and convictions, and your same desire to act . . .

Ibrahim was thirty-one years old and had lived a difficult life.

His mother, an extremely beautiful Jordanian woman, had met his father at a conference about atoms, in Amman, years earlier. They were both young engineers, cultivated and full of passion for life. His father moved to Jordan with his family, leaving Gaza to find work, and he was still looking for work when he married Salma Aziz Abd El Rahman. They spent a few years in Jordan, then left for Israel. The Fathi family, Ibrahim's father's family, had already returned there, and he wanted to see them again.

Ibrahim was born after three years of marriage. He was a

pretty, plump baby, weighing four and one-half kilos at birth, and he was always smiling and happy.

He lost his mother when he was five. She became ill, an acute form of leukemia, and she died after about a month of agony.

It is difficult to explain to a young child that his mother has died.

It is difficult because he has a hard time accepting it, understanding it. What future is there for a motherless child? How can a child grow without a mother's support?

Fathi tormented himself with these thoughts, and he neglected his son without meaning to.

Ibrahim grew without the guidance of father or mother. He was a taciturn child, misanthropic, gloomy. He had no friends in school, at home he did nothing but study and, in his free time, stare at the walls of his room.

Sometimes he approached his father's room and watched him praying, the slow, almost rhythmic movement of his lips, measured to the precise and singsong tempo of the prayers, or he listened to him recite the Qur'an, with his deep, dark voice, and sometimes it seemed to him that he was trembling slightly.

* * *

Ibrahim attended university. He enrolled in the law program, a bit because he didn't know what else to do. It seemed to him like a fairly useful course of study, which one day would allow him to defend the rights of his people, not only with violence, but also with diplomacy.

He wasn't a demonstrative young man, but to him, that seemed secondary in importance.

His father gave him little time; he would awaken and go to

open the mosque, for the dawn prayer, and he would stay there praying and praying, for minutes, for hours, without every growing tired.

Ibrahim was filled with pride every time he heard his father's voice, strong and amplified by the microphones, inviting all Muslims to prayer.

He was also struck by the fact that after having lost his wife, instead of losing faith, his faith was strengthened. This seemed terribly important to him and ended up reinforcing his own faith as well.

His father showed passion for only one other thing, apart from religion: war.

The war that had raged, before his eyes, from the day he was born.

The war that had killed his companions, his friends, his relatives.

The war that fed off blood and tears, and that knocked, relentless and strong, on the doors of the Palestinian people.

One time Ibrahim listened to his father speaking to a gathering of the faithful, in the mosque. He was twenty years old, and he admired his father, who, the rare times they spoke to each other, always reminded him to be a man, a man, strong. You have to fight, Ibrahim, you must be worthy, this is your house, this is your earth, this is the only thing you have. Defend it. At the cost of your life.

Speaking to that group of faithful, in the mosque, his father said, when the enemy enters your house and takes the clothes you are wearing, understand, and when he occupies the rooms in your house and leaves you a piece of hallway, what does it take to stand up to them, you and your family? That's what he told them, what does it take to stand

up to them, you and your family, and afterward, after they have taken your things, they say "Now we'll make peace," you see, and if you say no, are you a terrorist? Maybe you don't want peace? Certainly you want it, his father said, but
    there is no peace without justice.

Like that, he said, like that, closing his eyes, searching his mind for images of the Palestinians that were dying. Like that, he said, searching for images of his wife and his family, his country, he said,
    there is no peace without justice.

Then Ibrahim stopped, he forgot about his courses at the university, he removed his shoes and entered the mosque, sat down on the floor and joined the group of faithful while his father said:

"We are in the right, remember, in the right," and when he saw a shadow, even just the slightest one, on someone's face, a shadow of doubt, he said,

"The land of Canaan, remember, became the Land of Israel, after, remember, after the Israeli conquest in the thirteenth century before Christ, remember, this is our land, ours.

And Jihad is legitimate

legitimate

Remember, Allah told us that you should defend your land and your family, and if someone comes into your land and takes your house and lays claim to what is yours, fight, use their weapons, their plans, their actions, do to them what they are doing to you and that will be a holy war, a Jihad."

Then Ibrahim watched his father's eyes, his determination, that determination, and he felt fear penetrate his bones, because that didn't seem like his father; he seemed like a man devoted to his country and to battle, a personal battle, because his father was fighting the enemy within himself, in his mind, and what was that enemy?

Grief.

It was grief, which he fought within himself, because he had to be a man, always, no matter what,

And his father, with that look and that grief and that will to do battle was a man.

*   *   *

One evening Ibrahim sat studying, after dinner, he was in his room studying the notes he had taken at university, when his father entered his room, Qur'an in hand, and he stopped to look at him, bent over his papers, with an air so vulnerable, so young, and he saw himself at the age of twenty, still so insecure and so innocent, he saw himself again, and he clenched the leather cover of the sacred book.

Perhaps a sigh escaped him, or something, because Ibrahim turned and looked at him, and said:

"Papa."

He said it like that, only at that moment taking note of his presence, and then Fathi entered and stopped in front of him and declaimed:

"Don't consider dead those who have been killed on Allah's path. Instead they are alive and well looked after by their Lord, happy for what Allah, by His grace, grants. And to those who have remained behind, they give glad tidings: Allah, by His grace, grants. And to those who have remained behind, they give glad tidings: Have no fear, there will be no affliction."

Ibrahim watched him without understanding why he spoke that passage.

*   *   *

"Ibrahim, Ibrahim, wake up! Hurry!"

"*Allahu Akbar!* What . . . ?"

Ibrahim woke up suddenly and looked around frantically.
Facing him was his cousin Gomaa, frightened, in tears,
upset.

He was crying,
he was a man, Gomaa, a man, and he was crying, and he
shouted: Your father!

Ibrahim felt his stomach tighten in terror, his hands
suddenly grew cold, a shiver shook his body and he
burst out:

What? Where is my father? Where is he?

Gomaa took him by the arm and dragged him away from
his bed,

and told him

your father

your father

they ran together outside the apartment and raced into
the square, where there was a large crowd, they were
shouting, he saw women sobbing, children crying, he
saw everyone running, and then he saw his father
spread out on the ground

and everyone looking at him, and his blood discoloring
the square

the Qur'an stained

and thrown on the ground, open, the cover broken.

His father on the ground, all that blood

he had arrived in peace, with the Qur'an, he had begun
to recite some verses

condemning the soldiers, condemning their violence and
their brutality,

a crowd of the faithful had formed, who repeated the
verses, growing excited and increasingly furious,
all of them with their arms raised skyward, their cries
ever louder,
children who were jumping about, they too crying
Fathi kept raising his voice,
by now it was turning into a demonstration, the anger
was growing,
the young men agitated, the women swollen with hatred
the soldiers had realized there was danger of an uprising
and had intervened,
they had begun to shoot into the air,
but the people, by now accustomed to the roar of
machine guns, had continued to cry out, repeating the
words of the muezzin,
the soldiers, increasingly worried, then frightened,
Fathi waved his arm in their direction,
accusing them of sins of blood,
of sins of faith,
the crowd supported his voice with howls,
he was after all an old man, he was only reciting some
verses
but they had intervened, there were so many
and finally they had shot in his direction
maybe he had acted, urged on by the force of his faith,
believing that that would have been enough
but he ended up alone, spread out on the ground, the
Qur'an next to him
maybe he had gone off, leaving his son alone once again.
Ibrahim pushed his way through the people, moving
forward slowly
He felt as if he were dead

He felt as if all this were made up
It couldn't be true, his father wasn't on the ground
And all that blood had never been spilled.
He approached his father's body, he knelt down, looked
at his dark beard, his eyes closed, his lips parted
And he looked back over his twenty years of life, he
heard his father's voice again
pronouncing the words of God, with devotion
He picked up the Qur'an, that dirty and broken book, he
picked it up,
and he heard himself scream.

*   *   *

Ibrahim left the university
and began wandering through the villages of Gaza, for
years, the Qur'an in hand and a single idea in mind:
to be a man.
To be the man that his father had been, and to defend
his own land, to give peace to his own people,
to vindicate all those deaths,
all that sorrow.
Sometimes he would turn on the radio and listen to the
news, and he felt a fire burning within him, pushing him
to go out.
He felt as if he were going crazy.
It was 1992 and the Labor Party won the elections, so
that Rabin was once again prime minister. Being half
Jordanian, Ibrahim felt betrayed: as his father had told him,
in 1970 King Hussein of Jordan had unleashed the army
against the Palestinians, provoking a massacre. He continu-
ously turned over that Black September in his mind. He
couldn't think of the massacre that this had meant, and the

fact that in '85 Jordan was proposed as a mediator to resolve the Palestinian question. He barely mitigated his rage and his hatred.

The Israelis had withdrawn from the Gaza territory after years of occupation, but Ibrahim couldn't remove from his mind the image of his father, of the Qur'an, and of the last evening when Fathi had read that passage to him.

Ibrahim wanted to die as well, if this meant defending his own land, gaining a place next to God, and life and material possessions no longer mattered to him at all.

He only wanted to find peace, the peace of his own people
And that inner peace that he had been lacking for many years now,
but he could not forget that phrase,
he could not
there is no peace without justice.

That was the ninth village he visited, but it seemed the most desolate to him,
not a soul in sight, only some houses here and there, a small mosque
a few shops, many shut down falling apart,
he walked
he walked a lot before stopping,
stopping before a voice that was announcing the Zohr prayer
and so Ibrahim stopped and looked around
he saw a child trudging
he was holding a bucket full of water, he was carrying it on his shoulders, holding on with one hand,
with the other hand he held the hand of a little girl
who must have been three, four years old

no more
they both had tired, dirty faces,
tired
dirty
and they moved ahead with great effort, as if
as if every step cost them great effort
Ibrahim felt a weight on his heart,
a weight
that reminded him of the day of his father's death
and made him nearly lose his breath
the weight of awareness
Ibrahim knew that his father had suffered, suffered until
that last day
and his voice had had almost imperceptible tremors
every time he read the Qur'an,
and Ibrahim could bet that even that final day,
reading the Qur'an,
his father's voice would have trembled a bit
All this he remembered
when he saw the two children
so he felt compelled to approach them and speak to the
young boy, to say hello, hello, to meet his glance, both
frightened and threatening, to see his father in that little
man, in that grown-up little boy, and he saw the shyness in
his eyes and said to him, I'll help you, I'll help you, no, don't
be afraid, I only want to help you. But it was useless, no, the
little boy didn't want to give him the—who knows, maybe
he thought that Ibrahim wanted to steal it from him, and
then the little boy pushed him away with his arms. Ibrahim
stepped back, and the child hurried away, holding onto the
bucket and the little girl, he hurried off to get away from
that stranger.

Having finished the Zohr prayer, Ibrahim remained seated
on the ground for a few
minutes, in that place of peace
place of peace
For Ibrahim paradise had to be a bit like a mosque
only silence, protective and reassuring silence,
true silence
innocent
and the tranquillity,
and that perfection,
his eyes closed, he felt almost as if he were being lifted
up to a higher dimension, where his sorrow was only an
ugly memory
but this feeling vanished
the moment that he became aware that someone was
watching him
he felt that he was being watched and he opened his
eyes
he looked around and saw a man who was staring at him
it was a very tall and thin man,
his face lean and angular, thin lipped, aquiline nose
and very large eyes that seemed to clash
with all the rest of his face
he had the air of a mild and friendly man
and he continued to stare at Ibrahim, but without
hostility or shyness
rather with kindness
as if he were curious
but not wanting to make him feel uncomfortable
Ibrahim stood up and walking slowly toward the mosque
exit
he took his shoes and put them on, then, always with

measured gestures,
he went out
feeling the intense glance that seemed to pierce his
spine
then, he knew, I mean, it is a strange feeling, it's not a
premonition, it's not a coincidence, you know it and
that's all, it's one of those things that happen like that,
you cannot order it, and you simply feel it inside,
and in the end you are ready because you know that it
is about to happen
happen
that's it, he knew it, just like that, and perhaps with that
studied way of behaving he wanted to encourage the
man, it had come to him so naturally because he knew
that the man would speak to him
in fact he spoke to him
he did, and he said
Hello, hello, he said to him, this is the first time that I
have seen you here in the mosque, are you by chance
coming from another village, like that, he spoke to him,
moving his lips and sending words out flying,
words that seemed so light
and it seemed as if he had said something foolish to him,
something like lovely day isn't it, or your socks are such
a pretty color, some foolishness, but no, instead he had
said something important to him, no, important
and Ibrahim answered
my name is Ibrahim.

The very tall and thin man with the lean and pointed face
and the large eyes
was named Nedal,

and he was really only twenty years old, he was a young
man,
but he had this mature air, Ibrahim didn't understand
why, but he had this mature air
and his words flew
and he treated Ibrahim as if he were his brother
Nedal lived with his sister and his mother, his father had
emigrated to Syria
he seemed like a young man with great inner peace
It seemed strange to Ibrahim
that a person so young, so delicate
could be so sure of his role in life
It seemed strange to Ibrahim
He liked him a lot, Nedal
That day they chatted a bit and walked around a lot
Ibrahim was able to see that the village seemed to be
divided into two areas, one practically uninhabited, and
it was through that section that he had passed when he
arrived,
The other was where the people were concentrated
There, some cafés were open,
the gray, old buildings had thrown open side and life
rushed on,
even if almost by force, it seemed as if the days dragged
on in
eternal and inexplicable instants
And Nedal told him that like that, one day one might be
able to appreciate more, just like that, he said, you have
all this time, all this time, only now and then something
happens, but the rest of the time everything is suspended, a bit like death
suspended

and you are surprised to be alive, you are living, but you
almost don't notice it
He talked to him like this and the man increasingly
amazed Ibrahim
Nedal deserved to live a better life, Ibrahim thought, he
was a very intelligent person, but he had had to give up
his studies in order to work
Life isn't easy, Nedal told him, sometimes you have to go
along with it, right?
Somehow you have to go along with it
So the days passed by
Ibrahim slept at the house of an old man who rented out
two bedrooms,
but he spent all day outside, with Nedal,
they talked for the most part
or they looked for little jobs,
to bring in a bit of money,
they lived a bit from day to day, like that, and in wartime
this was perhaps the best thing to do.

*   *   *

One day Ibrahim and Nedal were sitting at a café,
they were playing chess,
when they heard distraught voices, which grew increasingly loud
they hurried outside and saw a group of soldiers having
a discussion with two men, their tone growing sharper,
and the expressions on the faces of the men arguing
growing harsher and more acrimonious, and before long
a small quarrel broke out,
there were four soldiers, and they seemed much more
sure of themselves, brash in their uniforms and

strengthened by the power accorded them by their rifles,
but to Ibrahim, the people seemed much more dangerous,
at which point Nedal and Ibrahim moved closer to the
center of the altercation and stayed there listening to
the cries rising from all sides, and they heard about how
those soldiers had shown up at the door of the mosque
to check on things, at least this was the excuse they
gave, that's it, to check that everything was calm, and
obviously the excuse wasn't convincing, but this didn't
matter, it didn't matter that the Israeli soldiers had no
reason to enter a mosque, nor that they did it with such
disregard and boldness, it didn't matter because they
were the strongest, the strongest, always
and Ibrahim was thinking this while his eyes showed
increasing concern
because the poor people always lose, he was thinking,
even when they are right
even when they are right
the soldiers, then, didn't limit themselves with stooping
at the threshold, but they went right in
with their boots
leaving mud and dust
on the pure prayer rugs
and raising their voices, interrupting and disturbing
those who were praying
because they wanted to check
that's what they said, just like that, wanted to check
what, Ibrahim wondered, what, but he didn't dare speak,
the tension was at its height, it seemed to fill their
minds, their hearts,
and it would blow up, it would blow up
in terrible fashion, they knew it and they were all afraid,

terribly afraid
the war, Ibrahim thought,
the despicable war,
Ibrahim thought
and then he saw what he knew he should be frightened
of, and it was something in the eyes of one of the
soldiers,
the one who was cockier, more arrogant,
it was what he saw in those eyes,
he saw something go off
like an inexorable and abrupt mechanism
that's it
the eyes of that soldier said
enough now
enough
the people began to shout, to say get out of here,
leave us in our country, our land,
get out of here
and leave us alone
and don't come into our mosques and don't ruin our lives
and insults and contempt spewed out,
also fear, on the part of some,
while the tension grew,
it was then that it happened
in an instant
a boy, he would have been about twenty, a young man
wearing a pair of ripped jeans and a kaffiyeh wrapped
around his neck hurled himself forward,
perhaps hoping to be a hero
to do something real, something concrete for his country
for his people
he hurled himself forward, in a moment

he stretched out his hands,
perhaps intending to strike a soldier
it was an almost invisible instant, no one had the time to
react, to do anything
except the soldier
the more arrogant one
who in a moment, with an almost mechanical gesture
mechanical
with the gesture of one who is accustomed to pulling out
his rifle
to shoot
to kill
with an almost mechanical gesture
mechanical
shot
it seemed that those instants merged into a single
moment:
the boy bursting forth, the shot, and the body that fell
back, beneath an invisible force
and the body that fell back
back
and the shriek of a woman, the shriek that pierced
Ibrahim's eardrums
it seemed that they were pierced
and at that moment Ibrahim lost his hearing,
it was only for an instant,
an instant or two
but it seemed like hours to him
hours during which he saw the blood spurt and the body
fall with a thud and the people running up and the soldiers stepping back, this time less arrogant, this time less
sure of themselves, this time with death in their hearts

with the fetid breath of death that enfolded them
that enfolded them all
and that scene
that scene
so damnably slow and infinite, and terrible and so
so
so true
that's it, that scene that seemed the saddest thing
sadder
than anything he had seen his entire life
the saddest thing
that blood spurting and the body falling with a thud and
the people running up and the soldiers stepping back,
the saddest thing
that woman's shriek and that expression of terror
painted on people's faces and that mass impotence
the saddest thing
and that village and that desolation and death so near to
each of them, every day, death by now had become a
common fact, such sudden death and such unexpected
death and such unjust death and so close, so abrupt
the saddest thing
and that world and those people and their country, their
land and their history and their sad history and their
destiny
the saddest thing
and all these thoughts in a moment, in a single moment,
to return to the real scene, where
there was a boy spread out on the ground, rather the
body of a boy, a defenseless body, with blood gushing
out profusely and cries that were growing more intense
and hatred that was being unleashed by the glances of

all those people
and the grief that suddenly took hold of them,
the moment when, it was a moment, it was a moment,
Ibrahim noticed a movement nearby and he suddenly
turned, ready for another misfortune, his heart swollen
with fear
And he saw Nedal who picked up a stone from the ground
And he hurled it with force toward the soldier who had
fired, with force
in a gesture that expressed all the hatred and the
exasperation and also the impotence of a man
and a people
And Ibrahim always remembered that look, he remembered it every moment of his life,
while Nedal picked up the stone and hurled it
and his muscles taut with the effort of the movement
and the meaning of that gesture
were all impressed upon Ibrahim's mind
and he knew in that instant the nightmares that would
follow him for his entire life
would follow him inexorably
and would cause him to die, die
die inside
Everything happened as if in slow motion, the slow and
precise movements
seemed almost programmed, the annoying sensation
that what was happening
had been decided already, and there was nothing that he
could do
that any of them could do
to prevent that boy from dying, that soldier from shooting,
anything from happening

Nedal hurled that stone and the soldier turned quick as
lightning and in time to dodge the blow with disarming
speed, while the stone fell into thin air, and two of the
soldiers raised their rifles toward the limpid and clear
sky and fired, the people, frightened, retreated abruptly,
they all tried to take refuge behind a car, behind anything
that might protect them, then a woman came out from
hiding and threw herself toward her son, toward the
defenseless body stretched out on the ground, crying,
screaming, sobbing *ebni, ebni!* My son, my son!, and the
moment the soldiers saw her pitch forward
they fired, all four
all four
they fired and the woman was struck in four different
spots, in the left shoulder, in the right leg, in the throat,
and in the neck
she fell to the ground and the blood began to well up
spurting out and at that point nothing could be done to
change things, it was all inexorable
the machine
the war machine had taken off
even then
an unexpected courage broke through from an uncertain
point within the heart of each of them, an extreme
courage, and there it was, hands, arms, they all picked
up stones, rocks,
and in an instant, in an explosion of cries, shots, hurling
of rocks
it all came to a head
Ibrahim heard himself howling
like he had heard himself when he had discovered his
father's body

Ibrahim hated that howl that came forth from the
darkest meanderings of his being and shook him to his
depths
He hated that howl
because it wasn't a human howl
Nor was it even the howl of a fighter, of a warrior, of
someone strong
It was the howl of one who realizes it is war,
because at this point he has seen too much horror,
because he knows that he will not be able to coexist any
longer
with the war,
that now has become part of his life
Ibrahim had seen war from the time he was born
And he would see it until his death.

Two of the four soldiers died, they were stoned savagely, as
Rabin said and as the
newspapers wrote,
but it was extraordinary how instead
instead
nothing was written about the boy who was killed
and the mother who was killed
but they said only that the soldiers had not acted first
and that when they had acted it was in self-defense.
It no longer mattered to Ibrahim,
because he had become so accustomed to the lies of the
newspapers and of his enemies
Ibrahim instead was distraught because he knew that
it had been Nedal who had urged on the others to begin
throwing stones,
it had been Nedal who had provoked everything,

and now Ibrahim wondered if he too were not in some
way responsible,
because he had been the one to speak to Nedal about
how fighting and violence remained their only weapons
against the Israelis,
he had been the one to tell Nedal that dialogue was now
only a faded possibility,
that the peace agreements had become only a utopia
And so was he a murderer?
Ibrahim, are you a murderer? ask yourself, good God,
ask yourself, are you a murderer? are you a murderer?
are you a murderer?
Would his father have been proud of him? Or would he
have been disappointed?

*　　*　　*

The stoning episode froze the strength and purpose within
each of them, it seemed as if the village had become immo-
bilized in a state of disconcerting apathy; people didn't
leave their houses and not a voice was heard out on the
street. Ibrahim spent entire days in bed, without seeing anyone, he refused to see Nedal for nearly a week, then one day
his elderly landlord knocked loudly at the door and Ibrahim
opened up.

Behind the old man stood Nedal, who entered quickly and
thanked the man, then closed the door behind him, and Nedal
stood still, standing straight up in front of Ibrahim and began
talking to him, saying that he had to get hold of himself, get
hold of himself because life

"Because life goes on, do you understand, Ibrahim? You
cannot let yourself become so upset this way! Not even I
wanted to kill them, understand, they were men and I

killed them, but Ibrahim, they killed our people, did you
see how they slaughtered that boy, did you see? Like a
dog, like a damned dog, and did you see the woman? Did
you see how they slaughtered his mother? Imagine if it had
been your mother, Ibrahim, your mother, and those bastards had slaughtered her in that manner, for God's sake,
Ibrahim, wake up wake up! They want to kill us all, every
one of us!"

"Nedal...Nedal...Nedal...oh God, Nedal...all that
blood, that blood. And how they were howling, before dying,
God, Nedal, how can I sleep at night? We killed them, it was
us...Nedal..."

"Ibrahim, I beg you, listen to me: it is our land. It is our
country. It is our holy duty, understand, we must, we cannot,
we must fight, save our children and try to give them a better future, not with the fucking soldiers who wander about
our villages to dirty our mosques and brandish their rifles,
the Holy Qur'an says so, Ibrahim, otherwise we would be
committing a sin. Allah tells us to fight for our land! And I
will fight, Ibrahim, at the cost of my own life,. I don't want to
live a long life and maybe die at the age of one hundred with
out being able to say that I have fulfilled my duty as a good
Muslim. Ibrahim, you understand, right? I had to throw
those stones, I had to!"

"Nedal...no, leave me in peace, leave me in peace, go
away, go away, go away...Nedal...I beg you, leave me
alone, I beg you, I beg you, alone, I want to be alone, I beg
you, I beg you."

"Now listen to me carefully! Be brave, Ibrahim! Be a man!
We must beat them thanks to our power of endurance! We
must win through our courage! Our fearlessness! Certainly
not with compassion, indulgence or weakness! Do you

understand what I'm saying? Ibrahim, do you understand? Answer me, please, tell me that you are with me! Tell me that you are with me, that we will fight and that we will make ourselves respected until we breathe our last breath and all strength has left our bodies and until we can no longer be of service to our country in any way! Ibrahim, tell me that you're with me for God's sake, Ibrahim, open your eyes, open them, Ibrahim!"

"No...no...I...oh God, oh God, Nedal. What God is with us, what God is with us. We slaughtered them, and that boy, and that woman. And all that blood, Nedal, oh God, Nedal..."

"Ibrahim, calm down! Calm down! I know, I know that you don't want to go on, but I understand you, I too can no longer look death in the face, Ibrahim. I too can't go on, but we have to resist! Ibrahim, those bastards slaughter us every day, our children, our wives, our mothers and our fathers! Ibrahim, you can't leave me alone! It is our battle!"

"Nedal...for Heaven's sake, Nedal...I...don't know, Nedal, I'm not strong, I'm not strong, I'm not strong...I'm not strong like you...I'm not strong..."

"YES! Yes, instead! You are strong, very strong, I'm convinced of it, you're stronger than I am! Stronger than I am! Stronger than I am! Understand? Do you understand, do you understand? Answer me!"

"I...I...I...Y-yes, Nedal, I understand, I-I am strong, strong, strong, I am strong, as strong as you, we will beat them...Nedal, I...I...am strong."

"Great, Ibrahim, great, I knew that you would understand. We are the best. I knew it, we are the best, we will win, we will dedicate our lives to this war, and we will win, okay? Understand?"

"Y-yes, Nedal, I understand."

"Tell me that you will never abandon me and that you will always follow me, in everything I do, and you will fight with me and we will struggle to the death. Tell me this, Ibrahim, promise me this!"

"Yes, Nedal...yes...I...I pro-promise you that I will not abandon you...ever...I will follow you, I will always follow you, and I will fight with you...and...."

"Promise me this, promise me this, Ibrahim!"

"And...and...we will struggle...we will struggle to the death."

*   *   *

Two years passed. Ibrahim and Nedal spent all their time together and their friendship grew stronger. That year, 1995, brought a decisive turning point in Nedal's outlook, and in some way to that of Ibrahim as well.

One day there arrived in the village some thirty or so Palestinian refugees, who had had to leave their houses because the Israelis had decided that their village was the headquarters for a group of terrorists...and so their houses had been demolished, and the village had become an Israeli base.

These people had no place to go, but in the village there was considerable support for them, considerable, since no one refused to take in a family. Indeed they were all quite willing to share those moments of sorrow with people less fortunate than they.

Nedal took in two siblings, a boy and a girl, named Gihad and Riham. Gihad was a boy of medium build, dark hair and gray eyes, always ready with a smile, unusually cheerful, frequently laughing. He was a likeable and sociable type, and for a while he took Ibrahim and Nedal away from the war. He didn't seem marked by the war as they, instead, were. He didn't seem unstable or insecure, and there was no sorrow in his eyes. About this, Ibrahim told himself that there were two possibilities:

either he had not yet seen the horrors of war, death, destruction, hatred

or he was a man with a tremendous responsive capacity, he was one of those people who knew how to take what was positive from things,

because he thought that nothing is ever lost if one still has the strength to smile,

and that strength must always be found,

and whoever manages to find it is stronger than those who instead do battle

and live a life of hatred and rancor

how do you think our enemies will react if they see that despite the sorrow, the losses, the horror of war,

how do you think they will react if they see that despite everything we still have the strength and the courage to laugh?

Laughing is for the strong, not the weak

and happiness is our anchor

Gihad always said

he was an optimistic and lively boy, and both Ibrahim and Nedal had so much to learn from him

even if he was only nineteen.

Riham, instead, was twenty-one years old. She had the same gray, penetrating eyes as her brother, a slender figure, long and extremely beautiful hair—for she didn't wear a *hijab*—and a very sweet smile that brought out two dimples in her cheeks. It wasn't the same as Gihad's joyful smile,

maybe because she was older, more mature, maybe
because she was more aware of the war,
in any case she too was spontaneous, not at all timid or
inhibited,
and she looked after her brother with great love and
with a sense of almost exaggerated responsibility for a
young woman of her age
Sometimes Ibrahim felt uncomfortable seeing her that
way, so involved with her brother, so anxious and worried
even if the reason for that profound attachment could be
explained easily
when they take everything away from you, house, work,
family,
a normal life,
that's it,
when this happens you grasp on to the only person you
have left like an anchor,
you fill that person with love,
with all the love you would have given to people who
at that moment
no longer exist.

When Gihad and Riham were still children, their family,
    their parents and little four-month-old twins,
    had been annihilated
    that day the tanks entered their village and the soldiers
    fired on all the people they found, women, old people,
    children,
    then went into all the houses, they set fire to some with
    the families still inside,
    in others they abused the women, stole money and
    destroyed everything,

they beat old people
and broke children's bones, but without killing them,
because people could survive for a long time with
babies, with children who grew up as invalids
and who burdened their families
people would end up hating those children, those young
people, who one day would not even be able to defend
their own families with the Intifada
who one day would not be able to fight like men
they broke children's bones and destroyed everything
When the boys and men began to rise up
the others had to withdraw, and they couldn't attack the
nursery schools and schools
because they would have done so
they would have done so
if only they could have.
Riham and Gihad were at school
and when they began to hear the shots, all the children
began crying,
crying
and the teachers shouted at them to throw themselves
under their desks
everyone on the floor, crying, terrified,
with a fear that gripped them,
many children fainted from terror,
some burst into tears,
Riham's eyes were wide open, and she trembled but not
because of the shots,
for her brother
she wondered if her brother in his class
was safe
far from her, far

while her mother told her every day, before letting her
go to school, to look after her brother
to be careful
and to stay close to him whatever might happen
Riham couldn't erase those instructions from her mind
and she felt she was a bad sister because she hadn't
fulfilled her duty.
After almost two hours of confusion and fear the teachers
began to go out from the classrooms, from the school, the
children didn't know what to do
Some children decided to leave and return home to their
families
and it was those unfortunate ones who, found by the
soldiers, were beaten up
And since the soldiers didn't have time to beat them to a
pulp
they sometimes limited themselves to breaking their
wrists, so they wouldn't be able to hurl stones
for their entire lives
so they wouldn't be able to defend themselves from
their enemies.

Riham and Engy, Nedal's sister, quickly became good friends.
    They were nearly the same age and they spent all day
    talking and cooking
    while Ibrahim, Nedal, and Gihad passed the time outdoors,
    in cafés or on the street, in the mosques, among groups
    of young men who were organizing themselves to create
    small militias
    that would be able to defend the inhabitants of the village
    The days passed slow and infinite,
    life continued,

even with sorrow and even with rage
it continued.
Ibrahim noticed that Nedal seemed very interested in
Riham; they were often together,
they talked, smiled and seemed to have an understanding
all their own
Nedal's eyes lit up when Riham entered a room, and
when she wasn't there
he always spoke about her
One night Nedal had a nightmare
He saw the people's cries and contempt
for the soldiers
and the people began hurling stones, hurling rocks, they
continued even if their arm muscles were stiff and their
bodies tired,
they continued undaunted
but the strange thing was that the more they threw stones
the greater the number of soldiers grew
one was added to another
to another yet another
and it seemed that they would increase infinitely,
they were all in their uniforms, clean and ironed, with
their machine guns in hand,
with their threatening glances
When Nedal understood that the only way to stop this
infinite multiplication
was to stop throwing stones
he let the stone he was holding fall
and he hurled himself toward his people, crying out,
imploring them to stop
but it was futile, futile
they continued, they seemed deaf and blind

like robots
Nedal began to shout and cry out of frustration and then
he looked for Ibrahim,
but he couldn't find him,
he couldn't find him
When he found him his cry was deep and rent the sky
Ibrahim was on the ground with blood smearing his face
and he was
dead.

Nedal awoke suddenly, sweaty and panting
He lay still until his breath became regular once again,
then he pushed aside the covers and got out of bed,
he went into the bathroom and rinsed off his face and
looked at himself in the mirror
his face was drawn, with circles under the eyes, his flesh
pale
he seemed weak and ill
what has happened to bring me to this? He wondered,
wasn't I once always calm and peaceful?
Where has that Nedal gone?
A little voice within him answered, a little voice insisted,
like an annoying sound,
because he knew the answer,
but it wasn't what Nedal wanted, so he thrust it back
inside
and he went out of the bathroom
at that moment he felt as if he were suffocating,
so he grabbed his cigarettes and went out
That night only the moon was in the sky,
ghostly clouds covered the stars,
the air was cool and he felt alone

silence and peace
Nedal saw a distant figure that was drawing closer
He went down the steps and went toward it and
discovered that it was the figure of a woman
When the moonlight illuminated the face
he saw that it was Riham,
she was wearing a sweater and a pair of baggy cloth pants
she was holding her hands crossed over her chest and
her hair was tangled
To Nedal she had never seemed so beautiful
He spoke to her before looking her straight in the face
before seeing her eyes
"Riham, what are you doing here?"
"I couldn't sleep, Nedal . . . Sometimes it happens to me."
"Me too, you know, I had a terrible nightmare, and I felt
myself suffocating, I had to go out and get a breath of air."
"More like a breath of nicotine."
"Well, the nightmare made me restless, I need to smoke,
to relax, you know. The smoke relaxes me. I know that it's
bad for you, but at this point I have been smoking since I
was thirteen. But . . . but were you crying?"
"NO! That is . . . no. I wasn't crying, I must have gotten
something in my eyes, but don't worry. Nothing important,
really. Did you see how beautiful the moon is tonight? Only
it's a pity that there are no stars. I like the stars a lot."
"Riham, please, tell me the truth: you don't trust me,
right? Yes, yes, that's it: you don't trust me. But why? I . . .
I think that . . . well, that . . . that is, that . . . I love you . . . I
think that I love you . . . "
"Don't cry, Nedal, really, don't worry, It's nothing, I . . . "
"Riham . . . Riham, you seem so alone to me, so powerless. Every . . . every time I see you there grows inside me

this need to protect you, I don't know how to explain myself because, but there, only seeing you cry makes me suffer and creates an unspeakable pain in my heart. I want you to be happy, Riham. I . . . I beg you, don't cry . . . oh God, but what have I said? Have I made some mistake? No, Riham, don't cry, I beg you . . . oh heavens, I . . . I don't want you to suffer. Riham, I beg you, Riham, look me in the face. Do it, Riham, raise your stupendous eyes and look at me. Look me in the face. I don't want you to suffer. Why are you crying? Please, Riham. Why are you crying?"

"Oh, Nedal . . . Nedal . . . God, Nedal, I . . . I . . . I am not crying . . . not . . . there . . . "

"Riham, why won't you tell me what is wrong? What pain do you have in your heart? Why don't you unburden your heart to me? Don't you trust me?"

"Nedal, no. I do trust you . . . you . . . you . . . well, when you speak to me I feel so close to you, so close and . . . oh, Nedal, I am crying because I am afraid for Gihad. I am afraid that the war will take him away from me. He is the only thing I have left now. I have had no family since I was eight years old. Only he is my family. I cannot think of losing him. I cannot think about it. He is my entire life, and it will seem absurd to you, but when I went to school, when I was small, my mother always told me to watch over him, and to protect him, to try to never leave him alone. Well, I see my mother who is telling me this even now, even now, and she is telling me to watch over Gihad and to not let anything happen to him. Nedal, if something should happen to him I not only would simply die of sorrow, but I would break the promise I made to my mother. I am only two years older than he is, but I think of him as a child, I have always seen him this way. You see it too, Nedal. The enthusiasm that he has for life, his naïveté. He is only nineteen. I am afraid of losing him . . ."

"Oh, Riham . . . I . . . God, how I understand your words. I am the only man left, my father has been in Syria for years, and my mother and sister are counting on me. I feel so responsible for them, but I also have an enormous fear of losing them . . ."

"This war is our plague. It has pursued our fathers, and now it pursues us, and it will pursue our children. Isn't there any way to prevent all this violence? Good God, isn't there a way to stop the sinners, the Jews? They are killing us all, why? Why does the rest of the world do nothing? Why do the other countries do nothing? If they would try to stop this slaughter . . . if . . . why don't they help us? Why do they stand still and watch, Nedal?"

"Because they are the ones who are our executioners, Riham. They, like the Israelis. We are alone in this battle, in this war. We are a people without peace, Riham, but we will have our peace alongside Allah. Those who now stand still looking will not rest easy on the day that they're judged. It is the only consolation that I can give myself. God is with us."

"Nedal, I think that you are a great man. I appreciate you a lot, Nedal . . . thank you."

"I . . . it is for you, Riham. I love you."

"Me too, Nedal. Me too."

*   *   *

A year passed without any unusual events touching the village or disturbing its relative tranquillity, and in that year the relationships among Nedal, Ibrahim, Riham, Engy and Gihad grew stronger. They became almost like brothers and sisters, each trusting in the others without reservation.

One morning, while the men were in the living room talking and the women were in the kitchen preparing breakfast,
they heard shots and cries
    and Ibrahim rushed outside with Nedal, and they saw
    people running shouting, terrified, without knowing
    exactly where they were going, Ibrahim tried to stop a
    boy he knew well, but he kept running
    Nedal ran toward the main street and understood the
    reason for such terror: the tanks were arriving. The
    tanks were signs of occupation,
    and occupation meant death, sorrow,
    it meant that there would be so many dead and few
    survivors
    Ibrahim saw a baby girl in a woman's arms, her eyes
    wide open, who continued to cry,
    it took all the breath she had in her body
    and she cried
    she cried
    It was a sharp cry, one that tore apart the heart, and to
    see that expression of pure terror
    hurt him,
    so much that he stood still until Nedal shook him violently
    and raced back into the house,
    Ibrahim followed him and in a moment there was chaos
    They told the others to run outside, right away, that the
    tanks were arriving
    As if she had not understood the seriousness of the
    situation
    Nedal's mother began to slip food into a backpack
    Her son had to tear it away from her and order her to
    leave right away
    A few minutes later Gihad, Riham, Ibrahim, Nedal, Engy

and the mother were running with the others, like the
others, they didn't know exactly where,
the important thing was to run and that was enough,
to save themselves
When they heard shots behind them they understood
that the Israelis had begun to shell the houses, and a
tear made its way down the cheek of Nedal's mother,
who no longer had the strength to run,
and she stopped,
Nedal and Engy began shouting at her to hurry, to run,
but the woman couldn't do it,
meanwhile a soldier who was shouldering a machine gun
had almost caught up with them, although for the
moment it seemed that he didn't intend to shoot
They begged her, they begged her to keep going,
but she said that this was her land, this was her house,
she had been born there
and she would die there,
she turned toward the soldier and shouted to him that
they were nothing but assassins and they had ruined the
life of an entire people, that they were sinners, that they
should have the heart to leave them in peace, to let
them live in the few houses that still remained
Then she made the mistake of screaming at him and
where is your mother now? Would you like it if I sent her
my son with a machine gun in hand? Would you like to
see my son throw her out of her house and threaten her
and so on, and the soldier pointed his machine gun at
her, and in a lightning quick instant so no one even had
time to notice
he fired
Nedal's mother fell to the ground and Nedal's cry, a cry

that had nothing human about it, terrified everyone,
maybe even more than the shot from the machine gun
Engy threw herself on the ground crying, to come to her
mother's aid,
Nedal hurled himself toward the soldier and managed to
fling away the weapon, Ibrahim and Gihad helped him
beat the soldier, who fell to the ground, struck by blows
and punches and scratches
Even before they realized that they were killing the soldier
they saw their companions running toward them,
so they began fleeing, but Engy didn't want to leave her
mother's body,
she is dead, she is dead, Gihad kept telling her,
there is nothing more to do,
Riham told her,
run, Engy, come, run, Nedal instead urged her
pulling her by an arm
but she cried out, cried, at this point distraught and she
didn't understand that staying there would mean death
Two soldiers fired, hitting their target,
one struck Engy, the other Nedal,
Ibrahim, shouting, hurled himself toward Nedal and
hoisted him onto his shoulders
Gihad picked up Engy,
and they began running again, with Riham who was limp-
ing, exhausted and confused, shouting, wheezing, alter-
nating flashes of lucidity with moments of pure madness
to shout with pure fear,
the drama of the moment seemed to envelop them
without leaving them any possibility of escape,
they were terrified
terrified

The bullets darted alongside them, grazing them, missing
them by just a few centimeters, and they saw death in
front of them, it seemed almost as if there would be no
salvation at the end of the street
there would be no salvation
but death,
death,
terrible and merciless,
and they were afraid of it,
they were afraid of it
and they knew they were so young
damnation, so damnably young,
and they knew that they had the right to live,
and it will seem absurd but at that moment Ibrahim
thought,
while he was running stumbling and feeling his aching
feet,
while Nedal's body was becoming increasingly unbearable,
he was thinking that it was unfair,
that he was still so young to die,
he still should have done so many things,
seen so many people
he should have become a man
as his mother wanted, he could not die
not yet
first he had to become the man his father had been
it wasn't fair that they weren't giving him even the
possibility
of proving himself,
it wasn't fair,
and it wasn't fair that those soldiers were pursuing them to
kill them,

kill them,
why, the devil, why?
What had he done to that soldier?
What had he done to deserve death?
And while he was thinking, it was absurd to have the
time to think
in a situation of this sort,
absurd,
perhaps it was a way to not let oneself be overwhelmed by
fear,
while he was thinking salvation passed in front of him:
a truck crammed with people, was about to depart,
damnation,
they had to make it,
they began to shout
wait for us,
wait for us
but the soldiers pursued them
and the driver preferred to not risk having the truck
hit,
so he started it up hands trembling, hurriedly,
the soldiers were arriving, he had to hurry,
even if his heart was weeping
weeping
to leave there those boys who were running and shouting,
shouting to wait for them
but he could not risk his own life and the lives of those
who were in the truck
he left
he left.
For a moment Ibrahim thought about throwing himself
on the ground,

he imagined throwing himself on the ground
at this point it was over
it was over
death had arrived for them as well
but
but at the moment when he already was surrendering to
death
a mirage appeared before him, it was a second
truck,
it was the last one that transported the people out of the
village,
the soldiers stopped shooting toward the boys and
aimed
at the truck,
it was crazy, but the driver of the truck didn't leave,
instead, he leaned out of the window and shouted
Boys, run! Run!
And Ibrahim, who a moment earlier had seen only
death,
understood that he had to make it,
that he had to make it, he ran, he looked to his right and
saw Riham running, wheezing heavily, her face purple
and sorrow in her eyes,
he looked to his left and saw Gihad with Engy on his
shoulders, his expression impassive, his serious
and frightened glance,
and by now the truck was a few steps away from them,
one more
effort
one more effort
and Riham with a leap was aboard the truck
then it was Gihad's turn

and Ibrahim was about to jump up
when he felt a hissing and a sudden twinge in his
arm, the pain made him cry out,
but he held Nedal's body steady on his shoulders,
he too jumped
and was on the truck
he was on the truck.
He was on the truck.

The moment he got onto the truck, alongside
Gihad, Ibrahim fainted.
The pain he had noticed in his arm was a bullet
that had pierced his skin.
The bullet remained inside, and his arm continued
to bleed.
He came to after a few moments, shaken by Gihad who
crying told him
Engy is no longer breathing
What on earth, help me, Ibrahim, Engy is no longer
breathing
Ibrahim noticed a hideous pain in his arm but he didn't
dare speak of it,
when he learned about Engy he forgot his arm
and seized with panic felt his friend's pulse
and his response was a tear that slid down, along
the rough crevices of his cheeks,
it was an expression of hatred that appeared in his eyes,
his features hardened, his jaw clenched,
and finally he whispered, looking straight into Gihad's
eyes,
looking straight into his eyes,
she is dead

she is dead.

Gihad hid his face in Engy's hair, while he was
shaken with sobs, and his back trembled with
violent tremors
Riham, facing him, had her eyes wide open, she was
in shock and didn't realize what was happening,
she stared at the blood and stared at Engy's body
but without uttering a word
without saying anything
Gihad shouted to the driver that they had some
wounded, to
go to the nearest hospital
In the meantime Ibrahim had moved Nedal so that he
was lying down, and Ibrahim was
checking the wound that was in Nedal's leg
Nedal had lost consciousness
but Ibrahim understood that he would live
if they could stop the bleeding
When he thought again about the body of Nedal's
mother, stretched
out on the ground, abandoned there,
with blood gushing out profusely,
he felt a lump in his throat,
his tears threatened to get the upper hand, and
he began
to breath deeply, trying to calm himself
when he looked at Riham again he realized that she was
still wheezing, her eyes were wide open
Ibrahim called Gihad
For God's sake, Gihad, look at your sister, something's
wrong, Gihad,
and Gihad, his eyes clear, stopped crying over

Engy's body and sought out his sister's eyes
with his own,
when he saw her wheezing
he said
Oh God, Ibrahim, Riham is asthmatic, oh God, Ibrahim,
we need to get her to the hospital right away
Ibrahim, do something
and the terrible thing
terrible
was that Ibrahim in reality couldn't do anything
anything
just as he hadn't been able to do anything for the
mother and
sister of Nedal
just as he hadn't been able to do anything for his own
father
just as he hadn't been able to do anything for all the
dead from
this war
and just as he would never be able to do anything,
except stand and look.
After about ten minutes, the longest ten minutes in
Ibrahim's life,
the truck stopped, the people who were inside, who
during
the trip had remained immobile, in silence,
began to get out, no one was looking anyone
else in the face,
Ibrahim rushed down, wearily supporting Nedal's
body and Gihad carried that of Engy,
Riham followed them, apathetic
The driver nimbly descended from the vehicle, despite

being, as Ibrahim immediately noted, a large, fat
man, with massive muscles
he immediately went over to Ibrahim and picked up
Nedal
effortlessly, then said to them follow me, we have to be
quick
he entered the hospital and ran down some corridors
the hospital was in chaos, nurses were running here
and there,
you could hear continuous cries, they were women who
lost
their children, husbands, parents
The man stopped in front of a door and went in without
knocking and inside there was a boy.
Ramy, the driver said to him, hurry up, these are serious
cases
The boy, Ramy, disappeared behind a door and when
he came back there were two doctors with him
They took Engy, they confirmed that she was dead and
covered her
with a cloth
They immediately brought Nedal into the operating
room, Gihad held
on tightly to Riham, who was still in the midst of an
asthma attack
A woman doctor took care of her, while a male doctor,
assisted by the boy Ramy, examined Ibrahim's arm and
explained to him
that before doing anything else they needed to stop the
bleeding,
and that they had to proceed with the extraction of the
bullet,

that it would be painful
but it would be over quickly
Ibrahim, as if in a trance, stared at the nurse: Ramy was
small and at least as thin as the truck driver was large
and fat,
he had thin black hair and a shy face, a friendly look,
around his neck he wore a necklace
with a heavy silver cross, he was evidently
a Christian.
Ibrahim liked him from the first moment, at least as
much as he
had liked the driver, whom he called over with a gesture,
while they were taking care of his arm. He told him that
he would be
eternally grateful to him, because he had saved their
lives and that he was a man whom Allah would reward,
then he asked him his name and learned that he was
called
Mohammad and he thanked him again, before his
tears and pain overwhelmed him.

"It's awful, Ramy, you have no idea what these kids have
been through, I can't take it any more, can't take it any more,
seeing this war while it kills my people, Ramy, I want to do
something, we cannot stand still here while they slaughter
everyone."

"Mohammad, I know. I see scenes like these every day: at
the hospital, and then when I return home, because my
nights are inhabited by nightmares. These Israelis are beasts,
beasts, they should all be killed. They take no pity on us. But
Mohammad, there is no need to take leave of our senses, not
even grief should make us crazy. We must vanquish them by

controlling ourselves. Look at Arafat, he can't do anything: he says one thing and his people do something else. We will never achieve peace with attacks and bombings."

"I don't give a damn about peace, at this point peace cannot be achieved! For God's sake, what do you think, that they maybe want to grant us some strips of land? They want to annihilate us all, that's the truth, and so I'm sorry for Arafat, but I have to do something. The Jews are calm in their houses, and we, instead, have hospitals full of people who are dying and villages destroyed, elderly beaten up, we have no choice but to go ahead like this! Listen, Ramy, I have decided, I must do something! Are you with me or can't I count on your help?"

"Mohammad, certainly you can count on my help, always!"

"You are a friend, Ramy. Mama, you should have been there when I pulled these poor kids aboard. They were the last ones left in the village, everyone had gotten on board, but the other truck, Semi's, didn't stop to wait for them, it couldn't, I mean, let's not blame Semi for this, in the end he would have put all the passengers in his truck in danger, understand, it was too risky. But when one of them raised his eyes, the one named Ibrahim, that was it. When he raised his eyes I saw them full of desperation, fear, all the impotence caused by this war. In his eyes I saw all our Palestinian brothers, and I couldn't help but go to him. Otherwise, it would have remained on my conscience forever, it would have tormented me every moment of my life. Yes, they riddled the truck with bullet holes, and for a minute I lost control of the wheels, but in the end those five got on board, understand? And then one of them died. God, I'm so sorry, a young girl, but there wasn't anything more to do, and another is still in shock, one keeps crying. They're operating on one, I think his name is Nedal. God, I don't think I'll be able to stand doing it much longer, running this shuttle between the villages and the hospital."

"But Mohammad, you're doing a great thing, you are helping lots of people, people faced with death, like today. How can you think of stopping?"

"The dead arrive every day, Ramy, dead upon dead, there are so many, so many, and then you see their relatives who cry and shriek, and the blood, and Ramy, I can no longer wash the blood off my truck. Understand? I have nightmares every night, I feel like dying as soon as I see those eyes wide open, those ashen faces and . . . why are they doing this to us? They are a cursed people, that's what I say, Ramy, they are a cursed people: they have suffered so much but now they are making us pay for what has happened to them. I mean, they have been persecuted for a long time, now why don't we try a bit of peace? Why do they continue to stain their hands with blood?"

"I don't know, Mohammad, I don't know. God will give them their just punishment. He will give them their just punishment. I have lost my family, in this war. There is nothing left for me to lose. I have seen it all, since I was born. I have seen missiles shatter the windows of the church in my neighborhood while we were there at mass, I have seen the faithful throwing themselves on the ground and crying out terrified. I have seen the steps of an elementary school bathed in blood and the blackboards soiled, the floor tiles where the blood will no longer wash away. I have seen soldiers of twenty beating old people and laughing among themselves, and I have seen . . . God, yesterday something terrible happened to me . . . "

"What, Ramy?"

"I was coming to the hospital, I was in a taxi, and in front of us there was an ambulance. At a certain point some Israeli soldiers stopped the traffic, formed a barrier and began to check everyone's documents . . . do you understand? One by one . . . they were looking for terrorists, they said, and meanwhile time was passing, the taxi driver was furious, a cry comes out from the ambulance, I immediately become frightened and get out of the taxi, I go take a look and the ambulance driver, a young man, tells me that they are transporting a pregnant woman. She was having labor pains, understand, and she had to go to the hospital to give birth. I ran to the soldiers and begged them to let us pass through. I told them there was a pregnant woman who had to give birth and who was dying of pain. And do you know what the driver responded, damnation, you know what he said back to me? He said let her die, that's what he told me, with that cold face, that detachment, that indifference. Let her die. I ran to the woman. Inside there were two nurses who were telling her to take long and controlled breaths, but she was screaming, it was hurting her so much. She told us to take her to the hospital, to hurry, that she couldn't stand it any more, but none of us could take her to the hospital. None of us. And this killed me, how was it possible that none of us could do anything? There must have been six or seven soldiers, we were a pack of enraged drivers, but we could do nothing . . ."

"What happened to the woman? What happened to her, Ramy?"

"Good God, Mohammad, she held out for an hour, screaming and crying. Then she began to lose blood, so much blood, and she bled to death. She died. And the baby also died. He died. And I wasn't able to do anything, while that woman clenched my hand, desperate, and looked at me, beseeching. Take me to the hospital, she said to me, and I . . . I didn't take her."

"Ramy, it must have been terrible. I can't believe that those bastards always get away with things like this. Stopping traffic when they feel like it and causing a pregnant woman to die. What bastards. They will pay for this."

"I have stopped thinking of a future for us Palestinians. Maybe they will annihilate us all . . . "

"Excuse me, excuse me, I . . . I . . . would like to know . . . where is Nedal?"

"Oh, she has come to! Hello, I'm Mohammad, the truck driver. I'm happy to see that you're better now."

"Nedal . . . Nedal where is he? And his sister Engy? Where are they? Where have you put my friends? And my brother, my brother Gihad, and Ibrahim?"

"Calm yourself, calm yourself. First of all, what is your name?"

"Riham. My name is Riham."

"Well, Ibrahim and Gihad are in that room. Gihad is doing very well, Ibrahim has only a wound to his arm. They're medicating it, but don't worry."

"And Engy? Where is she? How is she?"

"Well . . . Ramy, Engy, where . . . Ramy, you tell her that . . . well . . . "

"Who is Engy, is she your sister?"

"No, she's my friend. But where is she? And where is Nedal? They're okay, right? Are they alive? I'm begging you. You, or your friend, tell me where Nedal and Engy are. How are they . . . "

"Well, Nedal is in the operating room, but he should make it. We hope that he'll recover, but Engy . . . well, Engy . . . there was nothing to be done for her, she lost too much blood and when she got here she was already . . . she was already . . ."

"Dead? Dead? Oh God, Engy! Engy . . . oh my God, Engy!"

"Mohammad, hold her. She must have fainted. What an idiot I was. Help me, let's get her into the room."

"Good God! Ramy, we shouldn't have told her. Let's hurry, let's take her to the room, we have to bring her to. That's it, like that. Careful of the door. Slowly . . . slowly, careful. That's it."

"Bring a glass of water, some sedatives. She'll wake up confused and probably will go into hysterics. Help me."

"All right, Ramy, but stay close to her. I'm coming right away."

"Poor girl, look what a state she's in. God only knows what has happened. If only I could help you Riham, and tell you that Engy is still alive and well! How I would like to be able to do that. But I cannot . . . I cannot . . ."

"Okay, Ramy! Let's pull her up. That's it, like that, shake her and . . ."

"Aaah! Engy! *Allahu akbar!* Engy, Nedal. *Allahu akbar!* Why . . . why . . . I beg you, tell me that she is still alive! Tell me she's okay! I beg you! It can't be true, she can't be dead! I beg you, save her, save her! Aaaaah, why? God, God . . ."

"Hold her, Mohammad. Calm yourself, Riham, calm yourself."

"No, no . . . leave me . . . I want to die! I want to die! No, leave me, leave me . . ."

"Hold her tight. That's it, hold her. Stay calm, I'm giving her a shot now . . ."

"No! Leave me alone! I want to die! I want to die! Aaaah!"

"She's in a frenzy! Hold her. There . . . calm yourself, Riham . . . Everything is all right, calm."

"Yes, Riham, don't worry. There now, everything is all right, everything is all right, all right . . ."

"Hey, she has fallen asleep. Mama, she has been driven mad. It must have been a blow . . ."

"Death is always a blow, Mohammad. Even if you see it every day . . ."

"When she wakes up she'll have an awful headache and a large stone in place of her heart. It worries me, Ramy."

*   *   *

Ibrahim was upset

upset

he stared with resentment at the people who were taking care of him, as if they were the ones responsible for all his troubles

he alternated between moments of confusion and sorrow and moments of pitiless lucidity

during which he asked about his friends

and heard himself responding, every time, that they were all

well

even if he knew that Engy was dead

and that they were lying

were lying

at a certain point he became angry and began to shout he wanted to know the truth, the truth

and so they explained to him that one of the two women had arrived

at the hospital already dead

another was in a state of shock, even though she hadn't suffered

any wounds

and didn't have any injuries
as for the two men one was unharmed while the other had
just undergone an operation
but they couldn't say if he would make it
Ibrahim registered this information without reacting
or at least this was the impression he gave to the nurses
he closed his eyes, he tried to go back in his memory
to the moment when his life had some semblance of
normality
he sent back to the moment when he saw himself sitting
in the
living room, with Nedal and Gihad
while the cheerful voices of Nedal's mother, Engy, and
Riham echoed from the kitchen
Ibrahim felt he belonged to a family
Belonged to a family
A feeling completely alien to him, since
He had never had one
A father is not a family
At least he doesn't lavish you with attention and doesn't
try
to stay together as father and mother
A father like Ibrahim's had been only a father,
not a family,
and so, sitting there, together with people who loved
him, he could stay silent and not hear the depressing
silence of solitude, but the voices,
voices with different timbres, from time to time different
shadings,
opposing personalities, a mix
of people with whom he would have been able to live for
his entire life

he had felt, at that moment, that he was a fortunate person
a boy who had a roof over his head and a full belly
and the desire to laugh a bit
while his compatriots, many of his compatriots,
no longer had a house
no longer any desire to laugh, worse,
they no longer had a family
he felt fortunate, he felt fortunate, while he spoke
with his friends

"Sometimes I wonder if we will ever be done with this war, I mean, how long have we been fighting? Our fathers and our grandfathers and our great-grandfathers have done nothing else, and now we are doing the same thing, and who is to say that our children and grandchildren won't be doing it as well? Will they keep on going around with tanks and machine guns? Will they ever stop occupying our territories?"

"Gihad, those are all lovely words, but they have no intention of withdrawing, and don't think that we like fighting and risking our lives every day, but we are only defending ourselves, Gihad, or at least we are defending whatever we have left, some strips of land, if we were to stop they would take these too . . . they have never respected agreements, never, they have always and solely sought to occupy lands, ours and those of Lebanon, like in '78, they want to take everything they can, to create a Greater Israel, the extreme utopia . . ."

"But we cannot surrender to violence! I am fed up with seeing people dying and living in a state of war since I was born, every day of my life! I want to die in my home, at the age of ninety, in my sleep, not at twenty from a rifle shot! Things go so well, during these rare moments of tranquillity. There is an illusion that it is all over."

"You speak like that because you are only twenty years old, Gihad, and you feel young and calm and you believe that a false peace would be enough for you. But sooner or later you will have to open your eyes, Gihad, and I assure you that it is better to do it as soon as possible. Do it now, and start giving a hand to your people. Seriously, do you think the pacifist groups have ever done anything concrete for us? It's sad to say it, but the only way there is to save ourselves at this point is violence . . . and do you know what infuriates me? Those nations, the European nations, who criticize our Intifada but meanwhile don't give us the minimum help. If war is a misguided way, why don't they do something concrete? The truth is that war is a misguided way only when it suits them, and that's the truth . . . Ibrahim, what do you say?"

"I only want to win. Nothing else. To live tranquilly in my house, without fear that from one day to another someone might lay claim to my land. If violence is the only way that remains for us to achieve peace, we need to accept it and try to come off better. And then we need to respect justice. Because, as my father always said there is no . . . "

"There is no peace without justice. You have told me that every day Ibrahim, as long as we've known each other. Your father absolutely must have been a saintly man."

"Yes, he was. He thought only about religion, about Allah, about goodness and peace. He was always a man of the highest character. But this isn't enough, understand, it's not enough. If only it were enough to have faith, if only it were enough. When they come to your house to kill you, to take your possessions, they don't check how many Qur'ans you have at home or if you attend mosque. Faith isn't enough."

"Why do you talk this way? We have to have faith in God, and we have to believe in Him. He tells us to accept sorrows and to overcome them, to experience joys and give thanks for them, He tells us that those who suffer are under his protecting wing. We shall suffer on earth, and we shall find justice against our executioners once we are alongside Him. Why don't we believe in this? Why do we instead decide to become executioners, too? Our children who are dying are like theirs who are dying, innocent creatures! Why must we seek their death?"

"Gihad, listen: all this is very noble, but they don't reason in this way, they don't ask themselves if their God accepts their violence. They have suffered, they have been persecuted, and instead of learning from this, instead of having pity on us since they know pain, they inflict upon us the same tortures that were inflicted upon them. Instead of trying a bit of peace, for us, for them, they come to occupy our lands and open fire without even looking their victims in the face. If I were to find myself in front of a Jew, I would ask him: but aren't you afraid of God? And I would like to see, who knows what he would answer . . . "

"Nedal, I know that you're partially right. They don't hesitate to do to us what was done to them, and they have no pity for a people who because of them has forgotten what peace is, but you know better than I that they have everything it takes to win. How can we even hope that in the end, if there ever will be an end, we will be the victors? Isn't it better to try to avoid other deaths, other destruction, and resume with dialogue?"

"Gihad, we have tried the path of dialogue a thousand times, and a thousand times they haven't maintained the agreements. They have done what they wanted to do, going against the entire world. If there exists another way, we would have used it already, but believe me, there isn't.

You ask me how we could ever win, and I say to you: by believing in ourselves. Never ceasing to believe in ourselves, not even for a moment, not even if we are overwhelmed by suffering, not even if we are left alone. Our goal mustn't be anything other than this, to defend what is ours, our land. My father, up until the last day, always told me to have faith and to never surrender. To seek a path of dialogue at this point is like surrendering to their outrages and submitting to their will. Nedal, I do not want violence either, and if you know another way, tell me: I am ready to follow it from now on."

"I . . . no, Ibrahim, I do not know another way either. I don't know, it's just that a day comes when you wake up and see the sun and everything seems so beautiful and you ask yourself: why ruin it?"

"I, too, this morning . . . hey, wait! Do you hear? What are those shots? Do you hear them?"

"It's true! I don't want to even think about it. Come, Nedal, let's hurry, let's go see."

And in a moment it was all over,
the tranquillity, the discussion,
the normality of that situation,
the normality achieved with such difficulty
was all finished
and now
now he found himself there, seated in that hospital room,
between clean, white sheets, with other beds next to
him and other people torn away from
their lives,
with a tangle of thoughts and feelings that
confused him
and that made him a slave to what was happening,

he wasn't even able to shed a tear
for
Engy and her mother,
he felt his throat stiffen, his stomach turned upside down,
but he wasn't able to cry
but he would have liked to
but he would have liked to
perhaps his father would have been proud of him,
and the fact that he wasn't crying
but at that moment, being a man
didn't matter much to Ibrahim,
he only wanted to find a corner, within his space
of sorrow,
a well-protected corner and at the same time terribly
exposed to danger
a small and comfortable corner
and stay there forever
suffer there forever
and perhaps also die there.

He stayed in the hospital for a week,
Nedal's operation went well,
all he was left with from that episode was a
scar
and the immense sorrow,
the immense
incommensurable
unjust
irreparable
sorrow, which now occupied every part of his life
In an instant he had found himself without a mother,
without a sister,

without a family,
how would he have found a way to tell this to his father?
What would he have said to him?
That while he was working without respite in Syria
his daughter and his wife had been killed by some
Israeli soldiers,
that their family no longer existed?

And how would he, Nedal, manage to survive, without Engy, without her sweetness, her kindness, her cheerful and carefree way of life, without her sweets and her caresses, without her yelling—in reality more amused than admonishing—in the morning, when she woke him up, without her support, her sincerity, her loyalty, without her help in difficult moments, without the sweaters that she was able to make, without her joy in living, without those large and deep eyes, without her sweet and encompassing smiles, without her delicate way of understanding him, barely noticed, discreet and marvelous, and there wasn't even any need for him to say or do anything?

How would he manage to live without her?

And how would he be able to accept having lost his mother, the woman who had brought him into the world and who from that day on had attended to him and loved him without reservation, who had dedicated her entire life so he would lack for nothing, who had always appreciated him for what he was, who had said to him every morning, when he went out, to wrap up well, who in the month of Ramadan sometimes stayed up waiting for him, still fasting, even after the hour of Maghreeb, because she felt that she would never have left him to eat alone at a wonderful moment like Aftar, the breaking of the fast, that she would have been afraid for him every moment of this accursed, unjust war.

Nedal had to go on,
he had to continue to live even without the two most
important people in his entire life
how was this possible?
Riham was very close to him, she was in shock and held
her own grief well hidden in a corner
in order to seem strong and available to Nedal,
and spent the night crying until she was ill, alone
in the chill of that room
Ibrahim spoke very little and always kept to himself,
Gihad tried to hold the group together
because after that misfortune he had felt that death was
near
and he had smelled its odor
and seen its color
and now he felt a strong and almost painful need for
affection
Mohammad and Ramy spent a lot of time with these
four
And ended up becoming very fond of them
and feeling close to them,
because they already had lost their families
and they already knew what sorrow was
Ibrahim noticed that they were becoming a group,
a small group
and this puzzled him
Does sorrow bring people together? Does it really?
To him it seemed that sorrow unraveled him inexorably
dragging him
into the void and into the darkness of solitude,
and he felt that he couldn't react, perhaps he wasn't
able to

so he watched them and saw the small quiet smiles that
they
directed at each other
to console each other, to infuse each other with courage
to succeed in being strong
all together
and one night it happened: he dreamed about his father.
He easily dropped off into sleep, that night, an agitated
sleep, until
he saw himself trembling, bleeding, stretched out on the
ground,
and he got back up and looked around and looked for
some sign
of life
but there was nothing
and there was no one
it was an incomprehensible image of emptiness, of
nothingness,
that enveloped him
it was an end or a beginning
he wasn't able to give a color to that situation
white or black?
And then he arrived.
He was walking in that way of his, leaning slightly to the
right, his hands hanging loosely at his sides, he looked
straight at him, his head held high, small, infinite steps
And he was wearing his usual blue djellaba and had a
serious
expression
He never smiled
How many times had Ibrahim seen him smile? Once,
twice?

And with this expression, also a bit serious, he drew
closer, holding his gaze fixed on him, and when he got
rather close
he stretched out his hand, he stretched it out flat, with a
gesture both solemn
and affectionate,
Ibrahim didn't hesitate for a moment and gave him his
own, he
followed him
They walked around that emptiness
They surrounded it, they filled it, they were completely
one with the
emptiness
They were the essence of the dream
And in that instant Ibrahim felt so alive that it didn't seem
that it was a dream
And it was in that moment that
without withdrawing his gaze from his
he said one thing
one thing only
but which for Ibrahim counted for a great deal,
it was everything
he said, so softly it was nearly imperceptible
You are not alone.

*   *   *

Mohammad lived in a small house a short distance from the
hospital, and the day they were discharged he took them
there in his truck, he brought them in and said they should
treat it as their own home, because it was theirs.

Ramy came to see them at lunchtime, and Riham had pre-
pared rice with peas in sauce. It was all very good, and they

passed the time talking and discussing, not animatedly, not cheerfully, but together anyway.

Nedal, who always laughed and joked with Riham, and didn't lose an opportunity to tease her about her carelessness, was silent and limited himself to watching everyone. Ibrahim understood that his friend was thinking, he was thinking, and soon something would happen, something would change.

It didn't take long; a few days later Nedal called Ibrahim aside and said to him:

"Listen, Ibrahim, there is something I must tell you. Really, it's been some time that I've been thinking about it, and I didn't know just how. . . finally, how to tell you. You know that I love you like a brother, that for me you are every-thing, especially at this point. You are the only thing I have left. Well, I . . . "

"I knew it, Nedal, you haven't said anything for nearly a week, you stay there silent, you watch everything as if it didn't concern you. I knew that something was happening, but for love of God, Nedal, don't keep me waiting. What is it?"

"Well, I have decided to . . . I thought I would go away. I mean, go away, don't think that I want to disappear and for-get all of you, you can't get free so easily from old Nedal. But I can't do it. I feel like I'm dying, truly, you have an amazing ability to bounce back, but I can't do it. Really, I can't do it, I can't fake that everything is going well, and I can't smile, I can't find any peace with myself, I can't read, I can't do any-thing. I have tried, really, but . . . "

"But Nedal, what are you saying? Go away? Where? You would want to leave me here? I, you . . . but really don't you remember, we have so many plans, our future is together, I cannot think of doing anything without you, not even going out to buy milk. Why, why don't you want to stay with the people who love you? Listen, Nedal, I understand very well the hell that you are living. When I lost my father I was nearly crazy with grief and I decided to go off. And so I cut every tie with the past, I took my things and I came here, but it was useless, I met other people who taught me to love, because you cannot run away from sorrow, it follows you wherever, indeed solitude makes you feel its weight even more. I made a mistake, then . . . "

"Well, let me make this mistake too. Give me the chance to make a mistake, and then maybe come to tell me okay, I was right, but let me do what I feel like doing, even if it is mistaken . . . "

"Nedal, listen: we are all in bad shape. All. Let's talk, let's exchange small smiles of encouragement, let's try to get through the days levelheadedly. But in the evening, alone with our thoughts, we get overwhelmed by grief. Let's carry out our daily battle, but to win it we must stay united, all together, not get scattered throughout the villages, each blinded by his own grief. We cannot be losers."

"Well, I'm sorry, Ibrahim, but I'm not a winner like you, and so I want to lose, if that is what going away means. Don't try to convince me, please. At this point I have decided."

"Can't I do anything to convince you? Isn't there anything I can say to make you change your mind? You're leaving me? You're going away? And how do you think I'll go on? How do you think I'll get through the days, the nights? Who will give me a reason for going . . . for going on?"

"There are Riham and Gihad, and now Mohammad and Ramy, too. They will give you a reason for going on. They'll help you."

"But it's not the same thing. It will never be the same thing."

". . . I . . . know, Ibrahim."

An embrace, an embrace,
one tear, two
no, no, stop them, do something to stop them, but you
can't,
it's useless, it's a moment like that,
a moment that you cannot stop
Ibrahim hugged Nedal with all his strength he had in his
body and broke into sobs,
his body shaken by sobs,
tears blurred his sight,
an unspeakable pain squeezed his chest in a vice
everything he had built since the death of his father
collapsed in a moment,
everything he had built,
and his fragility exploded
at this point he was tired of sorrows and suffering,
at this point he was tired of war and blood
and he only wanted to live with a person
who reminded him of his father in the morning
who reminded him of his father in the afternoon
who reminded him of his father in the evening
who gave him a reason for living
who now was going away
and was leaving him there, alone and defenseless
faced with all his fears and his weaknesses,
another sob, stronger
sorrow is a force that destroys every resistance,
it sneaks in sliding between phobias and dreams and
thoughts
and feelings and emotions and truths
and when finally it is appeased
as when a work reaches a conclusion

and the work comes out, complete
finally ready
when finally it is appeased
it leaves emptied, tired and
incredulous
an embrace, a sob
while from the kitchen door another small
sob reached them,
no, not that of Ibrahim
nor that of Nedal
that of one who is suffering,
incredulous,
hidden Riham.

* * *

Nedal left two days later. No one dared try and convince
him, in part because his determination seemed so tena-
cious, in part because they all felt incredibly small in the
wake of the sorrow that such a young man could experience,
having lost his mother and sister, in part because something, deep down, told them that he would return

He would return

Perhaps it was only a faint hope, which they were mistak-
ing for certainty. Nedal looked at them one by one, with a
melancholy smile on his lips. Gihad, who continued to rub
his eyes, pretending that everything was all right, without
the courage to admit that yes, he was crying, yes, couldn't
hold back his tears, to give the illusion of being strong.
Mohammad, who continued to make witty little remarks and
to smile, to cheer up the others a bit and to ease the tension,
but in reality was suffering inside, like all of them. Ramy,
who seemed embarrassed and uncertain, who kept looking

all around him without resting his glance anyplace for more
than a moment. Riham who looked down at the ground and
didn't stop crying, who didn't stop crying for two days, who
sought comfort in Ibrahim, her eyes pleading, asking him to
somehow convince Nedal to stay, and finally Ibrahim
Ibrahim, who did none of these things,
who simply stared at him, spoke to him, confronted him
with implicit accusation in his glance, who didn't stop
speaking to him, looking at him, who seemed to be
telling him
you will lose all this, you will lose all this
but this wasn't his way to convince him to stay, no,
rather it was his own way to bid him farewell and to tell
him
you will return
you will return
At a certain point there was silence, everyone had
stopped talking at the same time,
Nedal smiled self-consciously, he looked around
And finally he said, measuring his words carefully
I will never forget you, whatever might happen
I will never forget you
And above all when we win we will all be one, us, those
who have lost their lives in this war, we will find peace, I
swear to you, I swear to you.
Then he had embraced them all, holding his hand over his
heart, to have them understand they would be there every
moment of his life, he lingered as he embraced Ibrahim,
they stayed pressed together for a moment that seemed
interminable
And mingling their emotions, their feelings
they exchanged a tacit promise

that they would see each other again
they would see each other again.
And then Nedal turned and left, his pace slow but certain, his back a bit bowed,
and then a cry,
the sweet but strong voice of Riham
Nedal
He turned just as she rushed toward him,
they clasped each other strongly
they remained joined
telling each other with the simple force of an embrace
a thousand words
crying and laughing
and finally separating
and looking each other in the eyes
one last time.

*   *   *

The first days without Nedal seemed to drag on with incredible slowness. Each of them awoke in the morning with a single thought: to overcome the sadness and the grayness that lay ahead.

Every time she let something fall or made a mess of something, Riham turned, expecting Nedal's warm laugh and his mocking words, his tender irony.
Instead, no one said anything to her
and Nedal's voice was only part of her imagination
Before going out Ibrahim, would say I'm going with
Nedal and then, absurd, he would remember that Nedal was no longer there, he was no longer there
And he lacked the strength to ask Gihad to accompany him,

because he knew that he was using him as an expedient,
and it didn't seem right to him.
Mohammad, while feeling Nedal's absence,
was always smiling and cheerful,
he made quips, he kept the conversations going,
he united the group
and when he went to the hospital along with Ramy he
noticed his absence,
silence reigned in the house.
Ibrahim began going out often and staying out all day,
he came back in the evening without giving the slightest
explanation to Gihad and Riham,
who were both offended and worried.
Nedal had always been a point of reference for each of
them,
and his absence disoriented them and frightened them,
it always seemed that something fundamental was
missing from every discussion,
every moment, every argument.
With time they began to have real problems
communicating.

If they were speaking among themselves, it was only to
argue, to offend each other and to hurl insults. Each took out
his own frustrations on the others, and they vented all their
exhaustion and discomfort with that perennial conflict on
the only people who in reality they loved and with whom
they were able to put aside the war a bit.

By now they had stopped speaking of peace, dialogue,
Arafat's strategies, or the attacks and suicide bombings;
they limited themselves to telling each other about the news
they had learned that day, an occupation in another village,
the death of a group of Palestinian families, two Israelis

wounded, three dead, the attacks, the violence. These were the heavy artillery of this war, for it seemed as though they wanted to hurt each other. They accentuated their words, the most tragic events, they concluded with macabre phrases, they openly showed their pessimism about the war's outcome.

They knew that the air that wafted through the house was saturated with tension, misunderstandings, and rancor, but they did nothing to improve things; it almost seemed as if that sudden departure had brought out the worst in them, and even though they were aware of it, the situation only worsened.

One night, in fact, Ibrahim didn't return home, and the next morning he returned around eleven o'clock, with a nonchalance and a tranquil indifference that was almost offensive. A furious argument broke out between him and Riham, mitigated with difficulty by the intervention of Mohammad, Ramy, and Gihad.

"IBRAHIM! Thank God! Thank heavens. What fear... heavens, heavens... Ibrahim, you are... you are... you are insensitive, that's what you are! A repulsive, insensitive egotist! Where the devil have you been? Huh? I have been trembling the entire night! Come on, Ibrahim! How dare you, how the devil dare you? You vanish, like that, without saying anything to anyone. But don't you have a heart? Huh? We spent an entire night looking for you in all the hospitals, the streets, everywhere, with death in our hearts, frightened, terrified! WHAT DO YOU HAVE THERE INSTEAD OF A BRAIN? I hate you! Ever since Nedal went off you have done nothing but be rude, boorish, indifferent! You make me... you make me... there, I don't even know if I find you pitiful or repulsive! Look, I don't even want to see you. I'm leaving because otherwise I'll spit upon you . . . in fact! In fact, wait here a moment: where the devil have you been? Huh? Or is it a secret?"

"Listen, you! First of all calm down and lower your voice! I don't have to account for my actions to anyone! How dare you insult me, raise your voice to me? When it comes down to it you are only a woman!"

"Ah, yes? And what the devil does this mean? Now you're also a macho pig! I have such contempt for you! I . . . you . . . "

"Shh, Riham, calm down, there's no reason now to . . . "

"You shut up, Gihad! And you, you boor, what do you dare to imply when you say that I am only a woman? Huh? Where is it written that men are better than women, or that they have a greater right to speak and cry out and jump and do what they like? How dare you, you boo . . . "

"I dare, that's what! I return home tired, exhausted, and a crazy hysteric begins to cry and insult me, how should I act? If you really don't give a damn about me and . . . "

"But Ibrahim, she didn't say that she doesn't give a damn!"

"Quiet, Mohammad! Even you, look how you, too, were roped into going to look for me! I stay out if I want to and you mind your own business! I'm sick of living with a hysteric who acts like the good little mother! Lower your voice, go to sleep, or do something else, and you'll be doing everyone a favor."

"Ah, so that's how you treat me? This is how you show your affection, your gratitude? I am always here sewing your socks and fixing your food and waiting up late for you and exchanging a few words with you and speaking kindly to you and making your bed and ironing your shirts and finally worrying when you aren't here, and you repay me by shouting at me to mind my own business and stop being a nuisance? Do you know what I'm saying, you . . . you . . . scoundrel, do you know what I'm saying? Now I'm really going! This way I won't drive you crazy and you can stay out all night and do everything you want without a crazy hysteric, as you call me, worrying about you! Now I'm going, so you can all be calmer and happier!"

"Riham, now you are exaggerating, we don't want you to go away, we are among friends, there's no reason to throw everything away only because of an argument . . ."

"Gihad is right, Ibrahim certainly has his share of the blame but you mustn't react like this"

"Don't interfere, Ramy! And you, Gihad, if you want to stay, stay then! I'm certainly not forcing you to follow me! In fact, I can see that you are already starting to think as they do. I am a woman and I have to stay silent, I cannot even become angry . . ."

"But I have never said this! Riham, try to calm down . . ."

"No I will not calm down! Do you realize that no one in here respects me? Do you realize that . . . you, Ibrahim! You! It's all your fault! You are insensitive! Whether it is this disgusting war that has changed us like this, or it is because your dear friend Nedal has gone off, you have become a monster! Do you hear me? Last night would have been better if you had vanished completely, that way I wouldn't have to worry. Look, I become enraged just thinking about the tears I shed last night . . ."

"No one told you to shed tears! Now you're making a scene and pretending to go, but this doesn't change things! You're pathetic, a neurotic who doesn't know what to do and who is picking on someone who has nothing to do with it!"

"I am not pretending a darn thing! I'm taking off now, and if I say so, I seriously mean it!"

"No, I'm the one who is leaving at this point!"

"No, my dear, don't turn everything upside down! Now I'm really fed up! You stay here and make the others, Ramy, Mohammad, and Gihad, die of pity, while you have the change. Because you know, Ibrahim, remember, that now they are maybe willing to put up with your craziness and your indifference. But someday even they will be fed up and then you'll find yourself alone like a dog! Understand? Alone like a dog!"

"That's what you say! You will be the one who is alone, shrewish as you are! And listen to this one thing: stop judging me! You can't even let yourself say these things! I am doing what I feel like doing, and if my behavior isn't okay with others that's their problem! If Mohammad doesn't want me to stay at his house, he only has to tell me so!"

"I have never said this, Ibrahim! Now you are exaggerating! As far as I'm concerned you can stay here your entire life . . ."

"If this crazy woman continues much longer, I won't stay here even for one minute!"

"No, my dear, now I'm the one who is leaving! Leave me in peace! So no one touch me! And you too, Gihad! Stay away from me! Now I'm really going! There! Where is my bag? Where are my things? There . . . everything is here inside . . ."

"Riham, what are you doing?"

"Ramy, don't interfere, leave me alone!"

"Riham, stop now. You aren't going anywhere, because . . ."

"Gihad, I'm not asking you for anything! Stay here with your friends and leave me in peace. There, now that I have gotten my things together I can get going."

"Riham, stop! Let's stop and talk about it calmly."

"Yes, Ramy, you're right, Riham, please . . . "

"Hey, listen, stop, come here . . . "

"Don't touch me! Get away! Cut it out! Our friend Ibrahim will be satisfied now!"

"Riham, I didn't mean . . . "

"No, Ibrahim, you meant it, yes indeed! Now the crazy one is taking off!"

"Riham!"

"Good-bye everyone, be well!"

"For God's sake, Ibrahim, see what you have done? She has . . . she has gone! Gihad, what are you doing?"

"Did you really think I would leave my sister alone, Mohammad? Did you think I would let her go away like that?"

"No, but you can convince her to stay!"

"My sister is stubborn and proud, if she says something she does it! The only thing I can do is follow her . . . where is my watch?"

"Gihad, don't listen to her tantrums!"

"Ramy, this isn't a tantrum! You said it all to her! Ibrahim insulted and offended her"

"Maybe because she was rude?"

"Ibrahim, she wasn't the one who spent the night out without telling anyone! Like you did, like children who go out to do the shopping and never return home!"

"Ah, then it's all my fault! You meant that . . . "

"Ibrahim, shut up now! Gihad, can't you even try to . . . "

"No, Mohammad, it's useless. I'm going now. Take care of yourselves. I have to run, who knows where Riham has gone."

And Gihad also left with his bundle on his back,

he left in a hurry,

once outside the house he began running down the little street until he saw his sister

and he called out to her, shouting her name, she barely
turned around,
without breaking her stride, and she looked at him,
then she turned away again and continued walking, but
more slowly than before,
it was her way of telling him that she was waiting for him
there was no more shouting in the house,
an unusual silence,
a sad silence,
Ibrahim with his eyes staring at the floor,
Mohammad who moved back and forth shifting objects,
straightening pictures,
he had nothing to do, but he didn't know what to say
he didn't know what to think
and it was better to keep his hands busy,
Ramy watched him, without knowing
whether to cry
or laugh
No movement at all
When Mohammad couldn't find anything else to do
he sat down in a chair and remained silent, looking around
Then Ibrahim raised his eyes and asked only, in a low,
hoarse voice, regret in his eyes,
he asked only
do you think she will come back
and none of them knew what to say,
because they were hoping so, they were hoping so
fervently,
but none could say
for certain whether Gihad and Riham would come back
they would leave an unfillable void
and the situation would accelerate even more,

if possible,
it was the end of something, that could be the end of
something,
first Nedal, then Riham and Gihad
was it now maybe Ibrahim's turn?
At that point Ramy asked, curious and annoyed,
he asked Ibrahim where the devil he had been
and the answer was precisely what he had expected,
out, like that, out,
to find myself a bit,
to think,
to reflect,
to hurt myself
You did it on purpose, right? Tell me the truth, Ibrahim,
did you do it on purpose?
Mohammad asked
All of a sudden he understood, all of a sudden he knew,
he felt an immense pain
for that young man,
you did it on purpose?
And Ibrahim answered
Yes.

That night Ibrahim didn't sleep
    He kept tossing in his bed,
    changing position continually
    then he kicked off the covers
    and got up, walking in bare feet on the cold floor,
    he left the room where until the previous night he had
    slept with Gihad
    and he went into the kitchen
    he poured himself a glass of cold water,

he quenched his parched throat and stayed there staring
into space for a while
Are you so afraid of being loved?
Are you so afraid of being loved?
He examined his hands,
the bitten nails, the fingers long and tapered,
like those of his mother,
at least that's what his father had always said,
and then he lowered his head, rested it on the kitchen
counter,
held it in his hands,
see, he was always capable of ruining everything
ruining everything
and it mattered little if he hated himself
more and more,
the problem was that in the end he brought discord into
the entire group
and he ruined the only beautiful thing he had managed
to build in his life
friendship
friendship
it seemed absurd, but in wartime, there,
with no more parents, without a family,
without any pretext, without anything solid and secure,
the thing he was left with,
the most important thing,
was friendship
they all leave, Ibrahim thought
Nedal has left, Riham and Gihad have left, I am left alone
soon Mohammad will ask me to get out of his house
what is wrong with me? What the devil is wrong with me?
Because the fear was so strong, the fear of loving

someone,
of loving someone so much,
the fear of noticing that you are creating a strong,
indissoluble connection
with someone
the fear of putting down roots in someone's heart,
this
it seems easy to love, it seems so easy to love,
but hating is much easier
hatred is such a gratuitous feeling, it doesn't take much
but Ibrahim had not succeeded in loving,
and being loved
in loving
or in being loved?
Isn't it maybe the same thing?
Isn't it maybe the same thing?
He felt a tear slide down slowly, being born and dying at
the same time
which made him blink his eyelids
the acute absence of Nedal
which caused sharp pains in his stomach
or was it his heart?
At this point he could no longer tell the difference, it
was only a question of suffering, which merged with the
confusion of that moment
Riham
in reality so dear
he had loved her like a sister,
and this had made him damnably afraid,
that reaction
the fact that she was so worried
the fact that she was so frightened

he remembered that, amid the cries and the insults,
she had said she had cried the entire night
and this, absurd, had made Ibrahim feel good
it had both hurt him
and made him feel good
the fear of having entered someone's heart
and the joy
if he had died
she would have cried for him,
she like all the others,
he had not lived in vain
and he was an important person in the lives of some five
people
didn't this perhaps mean something?
Ibrahim let a smile escape as he remembered all the
moments when
Riham had shown herself to be affectionate, almost
maternal, toward them
He felt mean and cruel
His behavior had precluded the possibility of being
loved
by Riham
and probably by the others as well
I am so good at ruining everything
damnably
good.

The next morning Ramy left the house very early to go to the hospital. Mohammad instead stayed behind to tidy up a bit, then he said that he would go see if they needed him at the hospital. Ibrahim asked if there were something he could do as well, at the hospital.

Mohammad stared at him resentfully, almost without
wanting to, and he told him no.

It was a bitter pill to digest, but Ibrahim tried to remain
impassive, and he answered that then he would go to look
for work in the village.

After Mohammad went out, Ibrahim prayed and then
he went out, too. First he wandered a bit by chance, then he
headed toward the only group of shops in the entire area. Not
far from the mosque where he used to pray he saw that in one
of those camps that usually were empty and desolate there
were some refugee tents. Who knows which village was taken
over this time, he wondered. He stayed to watch distractedly,
then told himself that maybe they needed him over there.

He approached slowly, a bit hesitant,
and immediately saw some rough cots made of wood
and dirty pieces of cloth
children, old people, women
wounded, bleeding, in agony,
crying, sad, confused,
but all needing help.
As soon as he arrived a very young boy approached him,
he said
We need help
where is the nearest hospital?
And Ibrahim answered that the hospital wasn't very
near, but that he had a truck at home and that he could
transport the wounded
The boy told him that they were all grateful to him,
extremely grateful
Ibrahim watched him, curious, he was a tall boy, of
average build, with a fair complexion, green eyes of
singular intensity, hair black as ebony, tousled, small

and well-defined lips, in reality his appearance was a bit androgynous but there was also
something virile about him, he was a strange contrast, his way of acting, of speaking seemed extremely brave, despite his young age, but when you looked at him with his beautifully shaped eyes, almost almond shaped, his delicate complexion, what came to mind was a female figure.

Ibrahim said he would be right back, ran home, where he knew that Mohammad had left the truck that day, and as soon as he got there he raced into Mohammad's room, opened up drawers, emptied pockets, even lifted up the mattress, looking for the keys. Finally he found them in a vase, in the living room.

He ran outside and jumped into the truck.

He had never driven a truck, but at that point it hardly mattered

It couldn't be that difficult, right?

He inserted the key in the ignition and pressed his foot on the pedal

his haste risked having everything go awry

in fact the truck lurched forward

then he took his foot off the gas and drew in a deep breath

when he tried again he was more cautious, and this time he succeeded in controlling the motor,

he got into reverse and backed out of the courtyard,

then began driving as he had never done before, with almost excessive care

at that moment he felt he was important

he could help people

he could help people who were suffering as he had suffered

and this was the opportunity that Allah was offering him,
after much time
when he arrived at the camp he braked and switched off
the motor,
all in all the truck wasn't as uncontrollable as one might
have thought,
instead, once he became used to it, it seemed even more
comfortable than a car.
As soon as he climbed out the boy from before ran to
meet him,
Quickly, quickly, he said.
Delicately but also, hastily, they transferred the
wounded and the dead, unfortunately there were some,
and it was terrible, those eyes staring into the void, wide
open, those pale faces, Ibrahim would have liked to have
closed them, those eyes, as if to give peace to those
people's souls, but there were so many of them, too
many, it was impossible to close them all.
They worked quickly, and Ibrahim's heart broke when he
heard the children crying, some because their legs were
almost separated from the rest of their bodies, or their
arms, or their hands, others because they saw that their
parents were being loaded up onto the truck but they
had to stay down below, they had to stay down below.
Ibrahim drove quickly, trying to remember the way to
the hospital
the young man from before sat next to him and told him
My sister is back there,
please save her
please save her
Ibrahim's heart broke even more,
because that boy had spoken with such fervor,

holding back his tears
but he had tried to seem strong and invulnerable
Ibrahim saw himself a few years earlier, because that
boy couldn't be more than five, six years younger than
he was
He saw himself a few years earlier
The only thing he had in mind
was that eternal phrase of his father's, be a man,
he knew that his father had not said it to him so that it
would become an obsession, and he hadn't said it to give
him a responsibility he would never succeed in bearing,
but it had ended up becoming one, an obsession, and he
was going crazy
he saw himself at that age
and he understood how fortunate he had been
to meet people who loved him
and he prayed that this little man might also find someone
who would love him and would help him face a war that
was too large,
too large for him.
Finally he managed to reach the hospital, some nurses
immediately ran up,
and all the wounded were unloaded first, then the dead.
Ibrahim ran inside and looked for the room where
Mohammad had brought him the first time, he entered
and found both Mohammad and Ramy there.
What are you doing here?
they immediately asked him
And he explained what had happened to him
The two went out right away to lend a hand as well
When he found the boy from before he asked him
Where is your sister?

He brought him into a sort of lobby where all the
wounded had been crammed, some on the ground, some
on the cots
The boy led him over to a cot and told him
This is she
Her name is Ashgan
Ashgan was bleeding heavily and was holding one hand
over her heart
Ibrahim understood that there probably would be nothing
that could be done
It was the same wound Engy had had
When the girl turned toward him, Ibrahim saw her face and
felt his heart skip a beat
He saw green eyes, identical, even in shape, to those of
her brother,
he saw the perfect complexion,
the tender and well-defined lips,
the oval face, the smooth skin,
you could see, without touching it, that she had the
smooth skin
of a baby, red silk
It was soft skin stained with blood
her hands with long thin fingers sought out
those of her brother,
the boy answered immediately,
he drew close to her and said
We'll make it, Ashgan, we'll make it
Ramy entered in a hurry, went toward Ibrahim and
looked at the girl
He said: she's in very serious condition, that's what he
said,
and he asked Ibrahim and the boy to help him carry her

out of there, they needed to take her to the operating room
the problem was that the nurses and doctors were
overwhelmed with work, so many victims from many
nearby villages were arriving
the enemy's advance was being felt clearly
Ibrahim found himself hoping with all his heart that that
young woman would make it
She was so beautiful, so delicate, and supporting her
body with his hands, along with the other two, he
noticed her thinness, her slightness
He found himself praying again
For a moment he even closed his eyes
then opened them again
they had arrived at the operating room, with Ramy he
put her down on the cot
then
he left the room and looked at the boy, he asked him his
name
Ahmed, his name was Ahmed
and Ibrahim looking at him felt a tremendous pain
the same pain he felt for himself
and he told him, he told him
She will make it, Ahmed, she will make it
knowing he was lying.

Ashgan died a few hours later, during the operation.
A doctor came out of the room, his face tired, circles
under his eyes
that lined his face, indelible, a shuffling step, a sad glance
Ahmed understood, he understood because he immediately became upset
But he asked, he asked right away

"So? So, is Ashgan all right? When can I go in to see her? When will we be able to return home? Has she said anything about me?"

"Ahmed"

"So, can I go in? she's all right, isn't she? Can I . . . "

"Ahmed, listen..."

"I have to see Ashgan, now, let me go, please"

"Sir, listen, I'm sorry, we tried to . . . "

"No, No! Ashgan is fine! Why don't you want to let me see her? She told me that nothing would happen to us, that we would always stay together! You can't keep me from going back home with her!"

"Ahmed, it's over, come on, Ahmed, please. Ashgan is now in a better place, where she no longer suffers. Ashgan has not abandoned you, Ahmad, come on . . . "

The tears, the sobs, the desperation, the sorrow, the impotence

and Ibrahim held him, held him close

he had known him for only a few hours, but he felt protective of him and he felt an affection he had never felt for anyone, he hugged him with all the strength he had in his body, he caressed his head, while Ahmed collapsed in sobs and held him

just as close

Ibrahim hugged him, he hugged him

because he knew how much he had wanted that embrace when he was Ahmed's age.

Ahmed didn't want to leave the hospital, during adolescence he had grown very, very close to his sister, they had always lived with Ashgan's husband, he, too, was killed during the occupation of the village, but they had been alone since birth,

so now Ahmed no longer had any place to go,
anyone to tell about Ashgan's death, anyone with whom
to share his sorrow,
and Ibrahim didn't take even a second to think about it,
he didn't even think about asking Mohammad's
permission,
he had decided already
that boy couldn't remain alone
that boy had found a family
Ibrahim waited until he fell asleep, then with Ramy's
help he carried him to the truck, he told his friend to let
Mohammad know that they had taken the truck to go
back home
and that there was a young boy with him
By now driving the truck was no longer a problem, two
trips had been enough to get him used to it
He passed through the village with one eye on the road
and one on Ahmed,
then, once he arrived home, he carried Ahmed to his
room and placed him down on the bed
he went back into the living room and sat down.
He thought about Ashgan, about the beauty of her face,
he thought about how important that woman must have
been to Ahmed,
he felt a sort of acute and profound melancholy invading
his heart, his mind,
he tried to get away from them, to detach himself from
these feelings
because feelings cheat you, they cheat you,
but he didn't succeed,
he thought about Ashgan and Ahmed and Riham who
had cried for him that night

and who now was who knows where with a lost and
powerless Gihad
and he felt not only melancholy, but also sadness and a
sense of guilt
he spent all afternoon thinking, sleeping, reading the
Qur'an,
without even the strength to go out
then finally Ramy and Mohammad arrived,

"Ibrahim, is she really dead? Is she really gone? Ibrahim . . .
is she gone?"

"Yes, Ahmed. In a certain way, she is gone."

That evening Ibrahim read the Qur'an aloud, while Mohammad and Ahmed stayed with their heads lowered, engrossed
in prayer, repeating in their heads the words articulated by
Ibrahim in his deep voice.

Ramy watched him, and he prayed in his own small way.
It didn't matter that he was of a different religion, it didn't
matter that his Bible didn't say exactly the same things as
their Qur'an. At that moment, they were all just the faithful
who were invoking the help of the same God, a single God,
who were asking for all that sorrow to be over, who were
asking for peace.

They heard a noise at the entrance, Ibrahim broke off,
Mohammad jumped up, but Ibrahim was quicker and flew
toward the door. He barely reached the entrance when he
suddenly stopped.

"Riham!"

"Ibrahim . . ."

"Riham! Gihad! You're back! Riham, come here!"

"Hey . . . slowly, slowly! I . . . we . . ."

"Excuse me excuse me excuse me! These have been the most awful twenty-four hours of my life! Riham, I was wrong, I, excuse me, I beg you, forgive me, will you ever be able to forgive me? Riham, I . . . without you, without both of you I cannot even think of living . . . "

"Ibrahim, certainly I forgive you, certainly . . . and know that I came here with the intention of asking your forgiveness. I mean, I . . . you are right, you can do what you want, I am only a shrew, and have no right to tell you what to do and what not to do, excuse me . . . "

"No no no! You have every right to tell me off and tell me what to do, Riham. Listen to me, I was wrong and that's it! I won't do it any more, never again, I promise you! Tell me that you will always worry about me and you will tell me off if I stay out late without letting you know!"

"Well, no, I want to apologize for having raised my voice and . . . "

"Now don't argue about who is wrong and who is right!"

"Mohammad! Come here. We were away only one day but it seems like I haven't seen you for a month. Where is Ramy?"

"Ramy, hi. Hey . . . Did something happen while we were away?"

"Well, yes. This is Ahmed. I met him at the nearby camp, they were coming from an occupied village."

"Hello! My name is Riham, and he is my brother Gihad. Gihad, come here, introduce yourself!"

"Hello . . . hello, Ahmed."

"Hello . . . are you friends of Ibrahim's?"

"Yes, and of Ramy and Mohammad. How old are you?

"Eighteen."

"How young you are. Well, we needed someone young here. I mean, we are all in our twenties, but we're so boring . . . "

"Riham, but where have you been?"

"Ah, traveling around a bit. We spent the night in a refugee camp. It is crazy, people are dying, people are suffering, but they never fail to help others. I felt so proud to be a Palestinian. Anyway I had to get rid of my anger. This time Ibrahim really made me angry."

"Well, Ibrahim, you don't know what a day it has been! She spent the entire time insulting you, and in the end she sat on the floor and began crying."

"Quiet, Gihad!"

"Come on, Riham, it can't be that you're ashamed of admitting that you started crying and said that you wish him a world of . . ."

"Come here! Wretch!"

"Here, we missed your cries, Riham . . ."

"What might you mean, excuse me, Ramy?"

"Ah . . . nothing, nothing. Why don't you fix us something to eat?"

"I'm just back and already you are treating me like a slave. I don't know if it was such a good idea for me to change my mind . ."

They smiled, and Riham went into the room that Mohammad had set aside for her from the time she had moved there. She arranged her things and returned to the kitchen to prepare the meal. Gihad sat down with the other men and after a few minutes of talk they resumed reading the Qur'an. As soon as they finished, he took Ibrahim aside and asked him to explain to him about Ahmed. And so Ibrahim told him his story.

* * *

It was the beginning of a happy period. Ahmed fit in well and quickly, and he ended up becoming the joker who made fun of everyone. He teased Riham about everything and played tricks along with Mohammad.

Ibrahim found work in a butcher shop and regained his good humor, he went out in the morning and returned in the evening, they all ate together and then drank tea, telling each other what they had done during the day.

Gihad had begun to go to the hospital with Ramy and Mohammad, but Riham wasn't left alone in the house because Ahmed was with her.

No one argued any more, the scars began to heal.

Ahmed thought about Ashgan every day and sometimes his voice grew dark and his face became serious, and his eyes lost their light; those moments might have lasted an instant, but that seemed like an entire day. Ibrahim knew that it was only a question of time. He tried to reawaken in Ahmed an interest in something to prevent him from thinking about the past and thus from doing himself harm, but it seemed that neither faith nor work nor affection could do much.

Ibrahim had understood that it was the new generation, They were all growing up this way, overwhelmed by grief and rage and it was hypocritical and unjust to criticize them when they were throwing stones or were killing themselves to become *shuhada*, martyrs. It was so unjust. How would he, Ibrahim, one day be able to berate Ahmed for the violence that would certainly be shown toward the Israelis in the future?

It is too easy to criticize those who make use of violence forgetting that they were victims before they were violent, that they in turn use violence to give vent to the anger that has risen within them because of the violence they have undergone,

it is the cycle of violence
difficult to stop
perhaps impossible to stop
but is there truly any desire to stop it?
Is there any interest in stopping it?
Ibrahim wondered about this often and he always concluded that the trap of violence
was convenient to too many
because it might stop, one day.
Sometimes, when his hatred toward the enemy became
acute, almost violent, he picked up the Qur'an and
prayed to his friends:
O Sons of Israel, remember the favors I have showered
upon you and how I have favored you over the other peoples of the world. He freed and saved them and they thank
him in this way? Killing their sons? But these are sinners!
At those moments Ibrahim raised his voice and his eyes
shone and he became upset in his ardor and didn't realize
that he was so similar, practically the same as his father,
and he also wasn't aware of the tremor in his voice
The others were almost afraid of him, but together they
listened as if hypnotized
It had an almost magnetic power, his voice, which
attracted everyone.

The war continued,
    it was 1996.
    The Jewish settlements continued, and
    in April, in Lebanon, there was a massacre of civilians at
    Cana. Ibrahim read in the newspapers how the number
    of Palestinian victims was growing,
    how the Jewish settlements were increasing,

how kilometers and kilometers of roads were being built
for the exclusive use of the settlements and the army,
how in the West Bank hundreds of thousands of acres of
land were being expropriated by Israel.
One day Ahmed arrived home angry and indignant,
saying that
it was obvious that the water they were always lacking,
it was obvious,
he had read that in Gaza the six thousand five hundred
Jews in the settlements were each consuming seven
times the water that each of the million and two hundred
thousand Palestinians consumed.

However, the boys began thinking less about the war and
the victims, as if to defend themselves from grief, and each
concentrated on his own life. Ibrahim began writing, he didn't
know exactly what his goal was and he didn't have a clear
story in mind, but what seemed important to him was to let
out his feelings and the daily anxieties, to avoid being rude
and aggressive with others.

He began noticing how he missed Nedal, his wise and
intense presence, his sincerity, his experience, and the
immutable, unconditional affection with which he had
flooded him, always, treating him like a brother and sharing
every moment, every situation, every thought with him.

Ahmed had found something of his sister in Riham, and
the two became very affectionate; he now accepted criti-
cism and advice with more compliance.

The month of Ramadan that year they all fasted together,
and Ramy wanted to fast with them, even though he wasn't
Muslim. It was a wonderful period: they spent much of their
time praying, reading the Qur'an, and discussing, always in
calm tones.

Ahmed began to have more faith in life, and he also managed to reacquire the faith in God that earlier he seemed to have lost. He stopped blaming Allah for what had happened to him and he stopped believing that faith had no role to play in facing his problems.

To Ibrahim it seemed that Ahmed was developing a way of thinking and being all his own, and he was as proud as if he had been his son, even if there were only seven years difference between them.

During that period Ibrahim wrote:

"I'm beginning to think that, after all, our illusions are a good substitute for real life. The real world is sometimes too harsh and we end up wounded: maybe searching for the truth isn't always the best thing. Especially right now, I realize how comforting it can be to still have dreams and hopes; they can protect you from what is out there. If I try, for a moment, to forget that our country is being invaded and taken over, and that my people are dying all the time, if I try to forget that the world just looks on passively, that people have forgotten about us, if I try to forget that someone is taking away the very air we breath, If I try to forget all this . . . well then, things seem to go well. It's strange, but I'm starting to feel resigned. I try not to show it because I'm afraid my feelings might spread to the others, but I no longer think we can carry on some sort of Jihad. Maybe we are condemned to suffer for eternity, maybe it is our people's fate to be without a land, maybe it isn't written anywhere that we will avenge the wrongs committed. Maybe, then, the only consolation is the next life, a paradise that only Allah will grant us. When I let myself think this way, the war loses all meaning for me, and the only thing that matters is finding a small space for myself at

God's side, along with the martyrs and the children and the women who have been killed."

*   *   *

"Ibrahim . . ."
  "Yes, Riham?"
  "I miss Nedal a lot. I think about him all the time."
  "I do, too."
  "Do you think he'll come back?
  "I don't know. . . I don't know."

*   *   *

Ramy began to stay out late in the evening, he left the
    hospital but didn't return straight
    home,
    no one knew exactly where he was going
    and no one had the courage or the insolence to ask him
    one day he came home extremely happy, changed his
    clothes in a hurry and then
    went out again saying not to expect him for dinner
    He also became moody,
    moments of incomprehensible euphoria alternating
    with moments of melancholy and immutable sadness
    they all stopped speaking as soon as he came into a room
    or they assumed expressions of discomfort and
    embarrassment
    He seemed like another person,
    sometimes he was cheerful and kind, made witty
    remarks and entertained the group
    but sometimes he also managed to be unbearable, he
    sulked
    and mistreated anyone who tried to speak to him.

One evening Ibrahim decided to talk about it with the others, taking advantage of Ramy's absence.

"Guys, I wanted to talk to you about Ramy. Doesn't it seem a bit strange to you, how he is acting?"

"Ramy? Why, what's happening? He seems quite normal to me!"

"Stop joking, Ahmed. It's important."

"Ibrahim is right, it's an untenable situation. We need to understand what is happening."

"Riham, no we don't, in my opinion. I mean, it's his life. Just because we live in the same house doesn't mean we also have the right to know where he goes and what he does! After all, he is twenty-two years old, he's not a baby, right?"

"No, Gihad, you're wrong. We need to understand what is happening, it could be something serious. It is our duty!"

"Mohammad, you say so because . . . "

"I say so because I have known him for four years! I worry about him, that's it! I don't want to stick my nose into his private affairs, but he is like a brother, or rather he is my brother, we are all brothers. I believe that we must find out what is happening to him. So . . . I see that the majority agrees. Well then, tomorrow I'll leave the butcher shop early and I'll go to the hospital, to wait for him to come out. Usually he leaves around five, doesn't he? So, I'll wait for him outside, and then . . . well, then . . . "

"Then what, Ibrahim? Do you realize what you're saying? You want to follow him! You have no right!"

"Ahmed, stop it. We are doing it for his own good. Then, I . . . well, I'll follow him and see where he goes. If I discover that he's going to a café to play chess or to some friend's house, I'll go back to the butcher shop and that's it, it's over. And if there is something else . . . well, we'll see what to do."

"No, no, absolutely no! Ibrahim, don't you see how dishonest and immoral this would be? If you insist, I will be forced to . . . "

"Forced to . . . ? What would you want to do, you wretch?"

"Well . . . I will be forced to tell Ramy what you are planning behind his ba . . . "

"You brat! Come here! I'll . . . I'll kill you!"

"Help, hold him back, Mohammad! Aaah! He's really killing me. Riham, I beg you, say something to him!"

"Mohammad, let me go immediately!"

"What do you want to do?"

"I want to give him what he deserves . . . I'll teach him to . . . "

"You won't teach me anything! You are not my father and you are not even my brother, you have no right to teach me . . . "

"You idiot . . . ! You're only a repulsive, spoiled little boy! How dare you? I am much older than you. You have to treat me with respect! Come here. Mohammad, I said to let me go! Let me go, I have to finish him off!"

"Mohammad, please, hold him back!"

"Say you're sorry! You insolent fool! Ask my forgiveness right away! Swear that you won't say anything to Ramy, otherwise I swear to God I'll break your ar . . . "

"Now stop it, Ibrahim, you're really exaggerating!"

"Don't interfere, Riham. Ahmed, say you're sorry."

"Sorry for what? I say what I like and . . . okay, okay! I beg you, don't hit me! Okay, okay, I won't say anything to Ramy, I'll keep quiet and behave well!"

"Mmm . . . let's see how can we teach good manners to a

brat like you. Okay. Now that we all agree, I would say that we can all return to work. Tomorrow we'll find out what is happening with Ramy."

The next day Ibrahim left took off an hour from work and, as
    he had said, waited outside
    the hospital for Ramy to emerge, staying well hidden
    behind a telephone booth.
    Ramy came out at the usual time and looked around
    Ibrahim hid himself better inside the booth while he felt
    more and more nervous
    And if Ramy had seen him?
    If he had noticed him?
    What would his reaction be?
    Would he also go off, as Nedal had done?
    Or would their wonderful friendship be shattered?
    When he saw Ramy hurrying toward the bus stop, he
    roused himself from his thoughts and raced to follow him
    He panicked as soon as he saw that Ramy was planning
    to catch a bus
    How would he be able to get on the bus without his
    friend, seeing him?
    He decided to give it his all and pulled his cap down on
    his head, hoping it would hide at least part of his face,
    and he moved forward slowly, always staying at least ten
    meters behind
    When the bus arrived
    he waited for Ramy to get on, then he raced forward and
    got on, too
    Ramy went toward the back and sat down in one of the
    last seats, Ibrahim instead remained up front
    They passed by a couple of Jewish settlements, full of life,

with shops, little gardens, people who were buying things,
going in and out of shops, young boys on skateboards,
young couples in restaurants, families on the street.
There the war seemed only like a distant event; a word
without meaning, a problem that didn't concern them.
People were well dressed and had the air of those who
have everything, money, health, power
it almost didn't seem real that a few kilometers away there
were such poor villages, where people were suffering and
dying of hunger, of cold, or even worse shot by rifles
it didn't seem real that the good life of these people and
the poverty of a people ripped apart by wounds and
sorrow could coexist
Ibrahim was so immersed in his thoughts he nearly
missed seeing Ramy hurrying to get off the bus
So he too descended in a hurry and pulling down his
cap over his face he watched Ramy
His behavior seemed strange,
he was surveying every street corner as if he expected to
be followed, he was rubbing his hands, scratching his chin
Ibrahim was afraid that Ramy had noticed he was being
followed, and so he turned and began walking on the
other side
he turned the corner, then stopped and leaned his head
out to see if Ramy was still looking behind him,
but Ramy was no longer there
Ibrahim felt himself panicking,
he began to look frantically, everywhere, then finally
noticed his friend at the end of a street
he hurried to catch up to him
he followed him for two hundred, three hundred meters
then Ramy entered a club,

Ibrahim hurried to follow him,
he too entered the club
there were psychedelic lights, girls scantily dressed and
boys smoking and drinking
Ibrahim looked around, amazed and curious
it had never crossed his mind that a few kilometers from
where he was living there might be such a place, so
different from the places where he and his friends hung
out,
in effect, seeing the drugs, the alcohol, the boys and
girls in all possible combinations,
boy-girl, boy-boy, girl-girl, boy-girl-boy, and so on
Ibrahim felt a deep sense of contempt growing inside him
for these young people who had lost their way in life
and certainly their religion, too
meanwhile, however, he had lost Ramy
he looked around until he spied him nearby, he was with
a Jewish girl
tall, very thin, short skirt and tight-fitting T-shirt, lots of
makeup, short hair, red, obviously dyed and full of gel
Ibrahim didn't like her, she was touching Ramy too
brazenly
it seemed incredible to him that Ramy would let himself
be touched that way by a girl,
and when she passed him something to smoke—it had
to be marijuana—he was afraid for a moment that his
friend, whom he knew so well, or at least thought he
knew so well, would accept
but fortunately Ramy refused the cigarette with a sharp
gesture and took the girl by the hand and led her toward
what must have been the back door
Ibrahim followed them outside the club

He found himself on a deserted street, and the two
young people were not far away
Ibrahim hurried to crouch down behind a garbage can
the two were talking animatedly, but in American English
Ibrahim made an effort to understand, dredging up his
own schoolboy English,

"Sarah . . . finally I get to see you, talk to you . . . you don't
know how much I have missed you, these days! I felt like a
caged animal. Tell me, how are you?"

"The same as usual, Ramy. Tired, depressed. Resigned.
Sometimes I wonder how you can be with someone like me. I
mean, you are so . . . so deep, sweet, intelligent, profound,
while I, I have nothing to give you. I am just a spoiled little girl."

"No, don't say that. You have a lot to give, you're unique,
really. This is why I would like to spend the rest of my life
with you."

"What? What do you mean?"

"Well, I . . . you know, I can't take these secret meetings
any more. I'm beginning to feel the need to be able to see
you, embrace you, every day, and . . . oh, well, I have a friend
in Khan Yunis and he has suggested I go stay at his house.
He's leaving for Cairo and will leave us his apartment. I want
you to come with me."

"Come with you? Me and you alone?"

"Yes, I would like to marry you, and have you become my
wife, and have every right to live with you, but to do this we
have to get away from here. So?"

"I think you're crazy! Khan Yunis, I don't even know where
it is! And then, what do I say to my parents . . . no, Ramy, I
love you but you are hallucinating! How could we go off and
live together? Then you wouldn't be with your friends, would
you?"

"Right, and I adore them, but everything seems so sudden to me! One day one takes off, then two argue, it seems that friendship is no longer enough to hold us together. Maybe it's the tension, maybe it's fear. Whatever, I want to leave with you. Excuse me, it was my understanding that your family is open. Can't you say that you're going away with some friends and nothing more?"

"Oh, please! What friends? Ramy, you're making me very confused . . . where did you get this idea about Khan Yunis? Maybe you don't realize the enormity of what you are saying. You set off a bomb and then get angry because I don't say yes to running away. Well, really, try to put yourself in my shoes!"

"Why, do you think it's easy for me? It's precisely because I can no longer stand this situation that I'm asking you to go away with me! Don't you see how beautiful it would be? You and I, alone, without any obstacle, without cautious glances or fears, without subterfuges . . . Don't you see how beautiful it would be to wake up in the morning and look each other in the eyes, and know that we are free, finally?"

"I don't know, I don't know. Please, Ramy, don't make me crazy now. I'm not saying that I don't love you enough to go away with you, only that you have asked me something serious and important, and I can't decide like that. Give me some time to think about it. Only some time."

"Okay. All right. But it will be a long and painful wait, Sarah."

You think you're building your own sense of serenity, around
    certainties
    so solid, so stable
    and when they collapse,

because sooner or later they do collapse,
and when they collapse
the abrupt return to reality
burning feelings that strike the defenseless soul
who previously had the illusion of having found peace
the abrupt return to reality,
Ibrahim felt like an idiot, how had he failed to understand
How had he failed to understand that Ramy was in love
it was love that had transformed him
it was because of that girl that he always returned home
in a different mood,
and he had not understood it
but in reality what he disliked more was knowing that
theirs was an impossible story,
that they would come up against innumerable difficulties,
theirs was an impossible story,
and Ramy was suffering
he would suffer
he, too, knew, deep down, how difficult it was to overcome
insurmountable obstacles
he, too, knew that he had been in love with a woman
whom he would never be able to marry,
and this was another unjust aspect of the war and the
hatred between the two peoples
Ibrahim had sensed the desperation in Ramy's voice,
the impotence, the rage
of a man who loves
but who encounters obstacles to his love
it was so sad that two people so young and in love could
not love each other freely
but love is born even amid war, love is the flower that
grows on the arid and desolate earth,

because love is hope,
but where is peace?
Accept it,
accept living in peace with your brothers,
whether Israelis or Palestinians,
or sons of the same God,
but where is peace?
peace?

Ibrahim knows perfectly well that the Israeli government cannot want peace, because peace means negotiations, it means compromises, it means interest and it means humanity and sensitivity. But the Israelis want land, everything. They want their Land of Israel. They want to create their utopia of Greater Israel, and they will not be content to allow the Palestinians to create their own state. They have never respected the agreements, they are trying to take everything, everything. God, the world doesn't notice, how can it not notice, Ibrahim wonders, and a voice within him answers that the world doesn't want to notice, it decided a long time ago, decided to act as if nothing were happening and to look away. The world decided to let the Israelis do whatever they want, it chose war, it chose death, it chose to abandon a people that has always been neglected.

Ibrahim knows what will happen, this is the second genocide in history. Those who hold power, those who are responsible for these deaths, have chosen not to learn from their sorrow, no, they have decided to torture another people just as they have been tortured, to make a desperate, unfortunate people pay for what they have suffered. People who have lost everything, except perhaps one thing, their faith, and this is why they are criticized, because they have given a name to their war, Jihad, because they have decided to not lose faith in Allah, and this is why they are criticized and killed and tormented.

And yes, the concentration camps. No, don't look for them with your eyes, you won't see them. These camps are in the minds of those Jews who support a lying government, who are re-creating the madness of a German chancellor, in the minds of those Jews who seem to represent all the Jews in the world, even if it isn't that way. Ibrahim knows, he believes, he hopes that they all aren't this way, an entire people cannot be this way. There are people who still believe us, who don't hide our tragedy behind illusions, but who look reality in the face, like that woman, that woman I saw one afternoon on TV at my neighbor Riad's house, that woman who in the name of the Jewish community in Sweden, her hand over her heart, declared that the government of Israel didn't represent them, that they were protesting the violence used against the Palestinians, that they were Jews, but not all Jews cursed the Palestinians, and not all of them wanted their destruction. And so those in charge don't represent the will of every Jew in the world, but they have the power to have us believe this, the power. They have concentration camps in their minds, but now they aren't building them in reality and they aren't throwing Palestinians inside because today the TV cameras would be there and because at that point the world would be forced to awaken from the damned torpor into which it has sunk, the torpor that has pushed the world to accept these deaths, because the world would be forced to wake up. God, peace can't be made with the dead. Ibrahim knew that the rest of the world looked at things as every Israeli did and this was why he had tried to make his friends understand that they had to watch out,

watch out for their feelings,
Good God, watch out for love,
love,
because it would make them suffer
one day or another
sooner or later
like now.

Going back in the butcher shop, Ibrahim thought again
about that short red hair
short red
short red
And poor Sarah in love
And poor Ramy in love
About Ramy
And that short red hair
About the short red hair
About the short red hair
To the point where he didn't notice that all that red he
was seeing wasn't the hair of that girl,
but his own blood.

"Ibrahim! What the devil have you done to your hand?
Look at this blood! Gihad! Bring me some cotton, some . . .
oh my God . . . gauze, disinfectant! Hurry! What happened
to you?"
    "Don't worry, Riham, it's only a bit of blood"
    "How is it that you're not worried? But look at all the
blood . . . it's a very deep cut . . . how did you do this?
    "Oh good God! What happened? Ibrahim!"
    "Don't worry, Mohammad, nothing happened."
    "Was it some soldier? Did you come up against someone?

Did they hurt you? Look at this mess! Oh God, Ibrahim, does it hurt?"

"Calm down, Mohammad, calm down. Everything's okay, I didn't come up against any soldier...And keep Riham away, otherwise she'll faint. In the butcher shop I let my mind wander and I cut my finger instead of the meat!"

"Oh good God! But did you cut it off?"

"Oh go on, cut off! What are you saying, Riham? It's only a deep cut, but the finger is still there, fortunately."

"Hey, Ibrahim, did you go, then? Nothing happened to you while you were following him?"

"Psst, you fool, quiet. Don't you see that Ramy is in the living room? Quiet, quiet, they're coming..."

"Ibrahim! Oh God, what happened to you?!"

"IBRAHIM!"

"Your hand! Oh my God!"

"Calm down, calm down. Gihad, Ramy, Ahmed...be still. I cut myself in the butcher shop, but now I'm fine, really. I just need some Band-Aids, or I'll bandage my hand, but I'm really fine, really, don't worry."

"God, but it's an enormous cut! How the devil did you manage to do it?"

"I was a bit distracted while I was cutting the meat..."

"Distracted? You're a complete fool! You can be distracted when you're cutting meat? Why, then, don't we also cut our nails while we're distracted, and then we can cut off our fingers!"

"Stop with the sarcasm, Ahmed!"

"Well, we can't all be wrong, after al...how can you work in a butcher shop and become distracted while you're cutting the meat?"

"That's right, think."

"Okay. Come, here, Ibrahim. And you, clear some space. Get up. Here, sit down here. Let's see . . . mama, so much blood. First we need to wash it away. You can't even see the cut . . . listen, Ramy, Ahmed, could you do me a favor? I wrote down some things that we need to buy for tonight, we have almost nothing left in the kitchen. Ibrahim, can you give him money?"

"Yeah, money, money. I go to work to shed my blood and you talk to me about money. Well then . . . here, take it, Ramy."

"Listen, Riham, send your brother with Ahmed, I am really tired . . ."

"I need Gihad to do some other jobs! Get up, go, Ramy, everyone has to do his bit!"

"All right. come on, Ahmed. Let's go, they're such slavedrivers here . . ."

"God, I'm so tired. Today at the butcher shop Sayd forgot to . . . Mohammad, they've left, right?"

"Yes, don't worry. Wait for me to get a chair. Here. Now are you going to tell us what happened. We have been waiting all day."

"Wait for me, I want to know too. Just a moment while . . . go on, Ibrahim, now I'm here too."

"Gihad, why don't you go peal the potatoes instead?"

"Pssst, Riham! I want to know what is going on with Ramy! Well?"

"So . . . then . . . he . . . I . . . that is . . ."

"Well? Can you tell us what has been going on with Ramy lately? Come on, don't make us wait!"

"Well, in reality . . . I . . ."

"But what's wrong with you? Are you going to tell us or not where you followed him?"

"But nowhere! At five o'clock I was outside the hospital, he left, he took the bus and . . . there . . ."

". . . yes?"

"He got off at a nearby village, where a friend of his lives . . . Yuri . . . Youmi . . . Youl . . . Yous . . ."

"Yousef? Yousef, maybe?"

"That's it, good, Mohammad, Yousef! Nothing, he went in the house, they left right away and went to a café, they played cards, drank some tea, talked to each other . . . and . . ."

". . . and?"

"And that's all! Then Ramy got on the bus, and I imagine that he immediately returned home, while I went to the butcher shop."

"But what time did he catch the bus to return home?"

"It would have been about six. Maybe six-thirty. Yes, six-thirty, more or less."

"And he got home before seven, so it's impossible for him to have gone anyplace else. Strange. Maybe he was aware that you were following him and he changed plans on purpose to confuse you! Maybe he wasn't going to Yousef's, but when he saw you he improvised a visit to his friend!"

"Don't speculate, Riham. No, no, I am sure that he didn't see me, I was very careful, and if he had seen me, I would have realized it. Trust me, he didn't see me."

"It's strange, Ibrahim. I, too, was convinced that something was happening with him, and I thought that today we would discover the truth, instead . . . I don't know. I could try to follow him, tomorrow, and see if he's still going to Yousef's."

"No! I mean . . . no . . . no, Mohammad, forget about it, really. I'll speak to him, I'll tell him that we have all noticed that he has changed and that maybe something is happening with him, and I'll ask him to explain what he has been doing in recent days."

"No, Ibrahim! That way he'll raise his guard, he'll find some excuse or other and we'll lose any chance of knowing the truth."

"No, don't worry, Riham. Now I'm beginning to change my mind. After all, we might have completely misinterpreted a moment of confusion for him."

"I'm not sure, Ibrahim, maybe Riham is right."

"No, Mohammad, I assure you that everything is normal. And the best thing to do is to trust in him. In the end, he is our Ramy, someone we know and love. We're talking about him as if he were an outsider, a boy we don't know. If it is something important, he'll say so."

"But . . . I'm not very convinced."

"Ok, Riham, let's trust Ibrahim. Gihad, aren't you going to open your mouth."

"No, it's that . . . I don't know, I thought that today we would discover something. Instead . . . I don't know . . . "

"Trust me, guys: I'll speak to him soon."

Ibrahim swallowed, he felt the hard and oppressive

weight of that lie

the weight of that lie

that burdened his heart and almost took his breath away

The anxiety was crushing

rage and sorrow mixed

into a single destructive force

as soon as he could free himself from his dubious

companions

Ibrahim went out to get a breath of air,

the cold wind lashed his cheeks, his tears were drying,

with the help of the nighttime breeze

but his torment didn't vanish, his pain
and above all his anger
he felt in part responsible for what Ramy was doing
maybe because he was older, Ibrahim felt almost overwhelmed by the responsibilities
he had toward all the others
it was too heavy a burden for a boy of twenty-five,
but the education he had received had made him serious
and conscientious,
perhaps even too much,
one who agonizes over the mistakes of others,
or at least those he sees as mistakes,
and who feels at least as guilty as they do
now he knew he had shut out any possibility of facing
this situation together with people he trusted and who
probably were as wise as he was,
but if he had turned back once he had done it a thousand
times,
it was a characteristic of his personality, both strong
and fragile,
harsh and sweet,
complicated but in the end so simple,
a personality that he now hated
what was there for him to do?
He felt so impotent
so alone
so fragile
He slept little and badly,
the next morning he awoke early and thought about
what to do,
then he decided to follow Ramy that day too
he had to know what Sarah's answer was before he

could do anything
at work he was distracted and listless the entire day
only he was careful
not to cut another finger,
then he left at five and waited for Ramy outside the
hospital,
he took the bus with him and got off at the same stop as
the day before,
he followed him to a cinema
Sarah arrived a few minutes later, this time she was
dressed much more soberly, jeans and a shirt, seeing
her like that she didn't really seem like such a bad girl
Ibrahim realized that the other evening everything had
seemed uglier to him than it really was,
the young people, Sarah, the club, the entire Jewish
settlement
sometimes it's easy to become overwhelmed by prejudices,
and Ibrahim was aware of this
unsure if he should follow them into the movie, he
finally decided to wait for them outside
He regretted this after a few minutes of boredom
The film lasted two hours and for two hours he
continued to think of the words he would choose to
confront Ramy
When finally he saw them leave he hid behind a truck
and followed them with his eyes
They walked some distance and finally entered a park
full of children who were playing and ladies with little
dogs and old people with newspapers
They finally sat down on a bench
Ibrahim hid behind a large oak tree, holding his breath
and being careful that no one might see him

"Nice film, wasn't it?"

"Huh? Excuse me, I was thinking . . . what did you say?"

"Nothing, forget about it. But I'd like to know what's bothering you. I have never seen you so cold. It seems as though you're not really interested in anything around you."

"Maybe that's how it is, Sarah. Maybe a film cannot help me forget the reasons I'm not sleeping at night, and maybe taking a walk can't do that either, nor can some words thrown out here and there, nor can a day of work at the hospital, nor even a talk with my friends. Is this enough for you?"

"Hey, why are you attacking me like this? I only asked you what's wrong! You might also treat me better, and stop using that tone, as if I were responsible for all your problems!"

"Well, you are! You are, Sarah. You're the one who made me fall in love and you're the one who now doesn't want to follow me and you're the one who is driving me crazy and it is your face that I see before I fall asleep. You are the cause of my problems, yes!"

"What do you mean by this?"

"I mean that you, instead of always acting so detached and indifferent . . . listen, forget about it. Really, let's forget about it. I don't know about you, but the last thing I want to do is argue. It's a rough period, everything here. Don't ask me to act as if everything were normal, because it's not. My people are fighting against your army, my people are dying every day, my friends have to deal with sorrows from the past, my girlfriend doesn't want to be with me . . . it's the worst moment of my life."

"Why would you say I don't want to be with you? I have never said that!"

"But you have shown it. And that's enough for me."

"I don't understand . . . what have I done?"

"I mean that with the first opportunity to show me how much I matter in your life, you have turned your back on me. To be important a person has to be able to make a desperate or simply a reckless, impulsive gesture. Love is impulse. It's irrationality. It's everything that you don't want to give me."

"Listen to you! How dare you? You don't know anything about me, then! I have never loved anyone as I love you, and no one has ever treated me this way! I don't know what your women do or have done for you, but don't think that loving means only becoming irresponsible and reckless! I take care also for you. I try to protect our love, don't you understand that you, too, are at the center of my thoughts?"

"If I really am, you have a strange way of showing me!"

"How should I show you, excuse me?"

"Khan Yunis, for example! What have you decided? Will you come with me?"

"Well, I . . . I haven't decided yet, really, you're not asking me something easy. I need more time, after all you only spoke to me about it yesterday."

"Time, time! It's only an excuse for not answering!"

"Think of it as you like. I have to go now. Every time we see each other it's worse and worse, it almost seems as if the only thing we know how to do is argue! Listen, let's see each other in two days, tomorrow I have something to do . . ."

"I . . . okay. See you in two days, at Sundays. At the usual time."

"Bye."

A cold way to part, cold.

Resentful,

delusion and weariness in their voices

to Ibrahim it seemed that their story would drag on

almost despite itself
and that it would overcome obstacles and difficulties
almost by chance,
that it was only a question of time, one day, two,
however much they might love each other
something was dying out
sadness, in reality,
a bit of sadness
in the end Ibrahim had never seen Ramy like this,
so heated, so passionate, suffering so,
like this.
He followed him while he returned home, he watched him,
he tried to understand what he was thinking,
his eyes dull, absent,
his gait slow, listless
he seemed drained of any energy,
incapable of reacting,
it hurt him to see him this way.
While he got off the bus and then returned to the
butcher shop he decided that he would talk to him
He had to, he had to
That very evening.

*   *   *

"Ramy?"

"Yes?"

"Listen, I have to . . . I should . . . well, I would like to talk to you, if you don't mind."

"Of course not, go on."

"No, well, it's a delicate matter. Maybe we can go out and talk a walk."

"All right, let's go."

"It's so cold. It's freezing tonight."

"Do you want to go back in and get your jacket, Ibrahim?"

"No, thanks, Ramy. Anyway, we won't be outside long."

"Okay. Tell me everything."

"Well . . . you see, for me it's difficult to have this discussion with you. I really don't know where to start."

"Start with whatever it is that you want to tell me. What is it about?"

"Well then . . . you see, Ramy, in recent days we have all noticed that . . . okay, you are always unpredictable, a bit moody, sometimes happy and witty, at other times euphoric and entertaining, yet at other times sad and melancholy, or angry and hypersensitive. We are . . . well, we wondered about the reason for these sudden changes in mood."

"Ibrahim, I can explain it to you, it's only that . . ."

"No, please. Really, I would like to finish. So . . . I . . . now, what I'm about to say concerns only me, not the others, understand?"

". . . I understand . . . but . . ."

"I know about Sarah."

"Wh . . . I . . . ho . . . bu . . . S S-Sa . Sarah . . . I . . ."

"Yes, now stop stammering. I know that you love a Jewish girl and that her name is Sarah and that you meet in secret and that you would like to go to Khan Yunis with her and leave us here because, how is it that you put it . . . one day we might no longer be here."

"Sarah?" But . . . I . . . d-don't . . . kno . . . kno . . . know . . . any . . . Sarah . . . I . . . Ibrahim, look, I . . . there is no one . . . that's right . . . I . . . you . . ."

"Listen to me carefully: I chose to cover for you and to not say anything to the others and to keep this fact to myself, but now I am coming up against you. Now that I have discovered your secret, you don't have to deny it, you only have to explain to me . . ."

"Oh, Holy God! What will you do now? Kill me? Do you want to kill me?"

"Oh, stop it. Don't act like a coward, good God, admit your responsibilities!"

"All right, Ibrahim, you . . . I . . . calm down, okay? Okay? . . . I . . . Sarah . . . oh, good God . . . but how . . . how did you find this out?"

"That isn't important, now. I want you to tell me how and when you met this Sarah for the first time and who knows about you. Ramy, it's important. Your story unfortunately is dangerous for both of you. So now explain everything to me, from the beginning."

"All right, all right . . . then . . . I . . . one day I went to see my friend Yousef, in the village . . ."

"One day when? Try to be precise, Ramy, it's important!"

"All right, but you won't say anything to the others, right? You won't say anything to Mohammad? Please, Ibrahim . . ."

"Okay, okay, go on, one day when?"

"I . . . a month ago, that's it, it was November. I went to Yousef's, you know, that pacifist friend of mine, and he told me he had gotten to know a group of pacifist Israeli university students. And so, he wanted to introduce me to them. At first I told him it didn't seem like a good idea to me, but then he explained that there wasn't any danger, and that it would be a great experience, and finally in the end he, you know, he convinced me, so I went with him and got to know a group of young people. And they were terrific people, really, I don't know . . . you have always told me that the Jews are all cruel and indifferent, but they were honest people, and they knew about what their soldiers do to us every day. Understand, they weren't like the others, and among these people there were some guys who invited me to go out with them. And so when I went out with them, I met Sarah. She was . . . I don't know if you can understand me, but she was so sweet, and she was friendly, and kind. She was different from how I imagined a Jewish girl might be, must be. That's it, Ibrahim, I think that in the end we're a bit prejudiced toward them . . . it's wrong to say they are all violent, all overbearing. So many of them aren't that way, and some don't even want the war. In any case yes, it's true, I want to go to Khan Yunis with Sarah. I am in love with her, and she with me. I don't think you can prevent me from loving."

"Oh, really, Ramy. Now I'm going to tell you one thing only. I haven't told anyone about Sarah and I have no intention of doing so. But if you really want to go away with her, I'm telling you: you're making a mistake. There are too many obstacles. You are the children of people that have been shedding each other's blood for generations. Her parents will never allow her to live with a Palestinian. I'm sorry for you, Ramy, and I'm so sorry for Sarah also. War isn't fair, and it also isn't fair that you cannot love each other. You have to be practical, rational also: do you think you can marry an Israeli girl like that, as if it were nothing? You can do what you like, ignore my warnings, but be careful, once you have made the mistake you will not be able to come back to me, I won't welcome you with open arms."

"For God's sake, Ibrahim, don't talk this way! Can't you understand that there can be a feeling that overrules all the rest? Is it so difficult to understand, to accept? Or is it only because you, from the heights of your wisdom, have never loved? I don't know what your problem is, but I don't have one. I love Sarah and I will marry her if I want to, and you clearly cannot tell me what to do and what not to do!"

"I'm just repeating to you, Ramy: don't ever come back to me. Not even when you discover you have made a mistake."

"What is there that's wrong about love? Huh?"

"Listen, Ramy, it's not love that is the problem. Love is a noble sentiment. I have nothing against Sarah, But I'm warning you: her parents will not allow her to love you. If you want to go off with her, do it. But you have to know that one day you will prove me right, but you will not be able to turn back. If you go with her, you abandon us."

"Why are you forcing me to choose?"

"You have chosen already."

In reality Ramy's choice turned out to be a mistake.
    One day Ramy came back home, in the evening, and
    began speaking to Ibrahim and told him,
    For God's sake, maybe you were right, you were right
    Today Sarah told me that she has changed her mind
    about the two of us and that she thinks we have different
    opinions about too many things, but especially about
    things that are too important, then she told me that in
    any case things couldn't continue this way, with us
    seeing each other in secret to avoid being attacked,
    maybe even killed, by her side or mine, it would be
    better to have a good Jewish boy whom papa and mama
    invite to dinner on Saturday
    she told me
    and then she said good-bye and left.
    Ibrahim looked him in the eyes with a hard expression
    and said to him
    I told you not to go back

And Ramy said only
Forgive me.

Ramy became very sad and anguished, he thought about
Sarah all day, and everyone at
home tried to leave him alone and not draw him into
their discussions and their shared moments. Ibrahim
watched him with a mixture of sadness and resentment:
in the end he had always warned his friends that it was
better to keep their distance from the enemy, even when
the enemy wasn't holding a weapon,
views too different
obvious incomprehension,
difference in backgrounds in ideas,
belonging to different ethnic groups but above all each
being so intolerant of the other,
it was impossible, impossible to love someone so different
and yet Ibrahim felt he was suffering along with Ramy,
because he understood the sense of loss, of pain that
was invading him
he understood because he only had to think back to
Ashgan,
that sweet and delicate face,
that veiled innocence,
those beautiful eyes,
sometimes he even dreamed about her
he dreamed about a love never experienced,
he believed that Allah sometimes would allow his faithful
to open a window onto what their life might have been,
that's what had happened to him
he had seen the Ashgan of his dreams, the one he loved
even without knowing her,

he had been able to see her eyes, even only for a moment
and then she was dead
without even being able to look him in the eyes
Ibrahim thought that it must also be a bit like this for Ramy,
he had seen Sarah's face
but without being able to love her
in her case he had also spoken to her,
he had loved her voice
but without being able to love her
maybe these stories continue in heaven
Ibrahim told himself
because in reality it was sad to think that there were
stories that began and ended in less than an hour
it was sad
just as Ramy and Ibrahim were at that time.
It was 1997,
a year had passed since Ibrahim, Riham and Gihad had
gone to stay with Ramy and Mohammad
but it seemed an eternity to them,
it was as if they had known each other for years and years,
they were like siblings,
it seemed as if they each knew everything about the
others,
and in fact at this point they knew each other's short-
comings, their good points,
they understood each other without even needing to say
a word
and the fact of being a family created a sort of immune
system
against the war
The Israeli troops occupied villages
and Jewish settlements populated by people from every

corner of the world rose up in swarms
The Israeli government said it wanted peace but in order
for them to free the Territories the Palestinians had to
stop the violence
The soldiers and tanks waited lazily for a desperate
Palestinian to commit a desperate act so that they could
take the opportunity to say that the Palestinians didn't
want peace
and in order to stay where they were other Jewish
settlements had to be allowed in
Perhaps there was a time when it would have been
possible to do something
Perhaps there was a time when the Israeli advance
might have been stopped
But now what remained to this people wrapped in their
kaffiyehs and in desperation?
A few strips of land
And even those few strips were being occupied, usurped
by the Jews
And even on those few strips
the holy ground of the mosques, the only place of
absolute peace, was being trampled by soldiers' boots
And even in those few strips
the cries of furious women who were arguing with the
soldiers were tearing to bits the silences
And even in those few strips
and above all in those few strips
war was raging.

* * *

One day Ibrahim was going to the butcher shop when he saw
a group of soldiers who were drinking beer and laughing, they

were blocking the entrance to a building and stopping with their machine guns some men who were trying to enter. When he approached and asked one of them what was happening, he heard them answer that it was considered a building of subversives and thus dangerous for the Jewish settlements in nearby areas, that the soldiers had received an order to search it and to prevent anyone from entering. The man explained to Ibrahim that it was a simple task and that it was only a bank. The soldiers had received an order to knock down the building and to shoot anyone who tried to prevent them.

A frustrated expression and a bitter smile crossed Ibrahim's face.

While he looked at those armed young men who were scarcely over twenty years of age, indeed some seemed no older than Ahmed.

At a certain point a girl arrived, tall and thin with long curly hair who attracted the attention of the soldiers, fluttering a sheet of paper

These are two hundred fifty signatures of people in favor of peace who have stated they have never picked up a stone and nor do they want to do so in the future,

these men only want to come in to work and you instead are using violence,

arrogance,

why violence? We want peace,

we don't want war

why are you destroying this building

where many men work?

Why are you shooting my people?

We want peace

But we no longer know how to defend ourselves

How to defend ourselves from you

These are two hundred fifty signatures and I am sure I
can get another two hundred fifty and still another two
hundred fifty, but then it's up to you
But then you must put an end to the violence
Why are you shooting people?
The soldier laughed and said
I am only following orders.

The girl's name was Yasmin,
    she was a doctor, or at least she had been one,
    she was thirty-one years old and four years earlier she
    had been arrested by the Israeli government because
    after a shooting in her village,
    she had found herself in an area totally occupied by the
    Jewish troops
    she had stepped in to aid the wounded and the dead
    Some Israeli police had arrived, they had arrested her
    and two other doctors,
    the doctors had already been arrested in the past for
    having given aid in Jordan and in Lebanon, after the
    massacres of the Palestinian refugees,
    all three were arrested and held in prison for a year,
    when Yasmin returned to her village she no longer found
    her house, it had been leveled, and no one in her family
    was left,
    she tried to rebuild her existence and to smile again,
    and then she joined a campaign against the war started
    up by a group of Palestinian students,
    now she was pleading the cause of her people, peace,
    nonviolence, dialogue
    Ibrahim, talking to her while he went to the butcher shop,
    told her that certainly that was a noble cause and her

ideals were noble
but they wouldn't come to anything against the Israelis
look, he told her, only look at those soldiers,
think about how that young man answered you
I am following orders
they are insensitive to the pain of our people and even
of their own,
even when all the world prays, begs, imposes agreements
they, heads high, get up from the negotiating table
and say no.
No.
And with that simple no they kill hundreds of children
And with that simple no they condemn our people to
eternal suffering
Yasmin, you can desire peace as much as you want
But if the other side is deaf to your pleas for peace
it comes to nothing,
understand? I, we, are not born with a desire for revenge
and violence
but it becomes part of us
when even our efforts at patience explode
Yasmin, you are a sweet and intelligent girl
But that's not enough.
Against them it's not enough.

Saying good-bye to Yasmin, Ibrahim hurried to go to the
butcher shop.
He was late,
but while he was walking he saw in the camp where he
had found Ahmed and the other refugees
a large number of men and children
he approached and stayed watching

there was a military course set up, built from little wood
branches, tires, ropes, rudimentary instruments
and some children in military uniforms, with fake
machine guns and pistols, who were reciting verses from
the Qur'an celebrating Jihad
the children were running, jumping, crawling, and doing
all this pointing their weapons at imaginary enemies,
when they completed the course the stopped in front of
the crowd that was urging them on, praising them
they stopped, thrust out their little chests, held together
their slender legs and raised their eyes proudly and
shouted, and their voices, absurd, almost brought fear
and almost succeeded in being threatening
threatening
they shouted
FIGHT FOR THE CAUSE OF ALLAH AGAINST THOSE WHO ARE
FIGHTING AGAINST YOU! KILL THEM WHEREVER YOU
ENCOUNTER THEM, AND CUT THEM DOWN FROM WHEREVER
THEY HAVE CUT YOU DOWN!
IF THEY SET UPON YOU, KILL THEM!
AND DO NOT SAY THAT THOSE WHO HAVE BEEN KILLED ON
THE PATH OF ALLAH ARE DEAD,
INSTEAD THEY ARE ALIVE
AND YOU ARE NOT AWARE OF THEM!
They shouted with all the breath they had in their bodies,
holding their rifles pointed toward the sky,
with a proud expression,
an aggressive glance
sometimes they laughed
their fathers were watching them proudly, the crowd
urged them on and at that moment Ibrahim felt like
crying, he saw those children with no way out,

the ideas that were being thrust into their heads
at that tender age
they couldn't be more than seven, eight, nine years old,
they were dedicating all their lives to their people
they were dedicating all their lives to hating the enemy
and to fighting him
and to praying alongside a rifle,
and they were already condemned at that age,
condemned to a life of violence
and their death was already written, their end already
decided,
they were prisoners of a chain that would never be broken
they were prisoners of violence
they had lost their freedom
any type of freedom.
Opposing emotions,
Opposing emotions
because he didn't feel he could condemn the parents of
those children
Ibrahim could not condemn those people
because they in turn, the parents of those children, had
grown up overwhelmed by grief,
overwhelmed by hatred,
how could he judge them?
How could he condemn them?
A child whose parents have been shot before his eyes
will have a twisted mind forever
he will be tormented by a yearning for vendetta
he will be tormented by hatred,
insistent,
perpetual,
violent,

he will be tormented and will have no choice but to be
converted to a life of hatred
and to raise his children in the same manner
At this point a seed of evil
had planted itself among them
and you couldn't do anything to fight it
Ibrahim shifted his glance away from that scene
It hurt him to think that in the end
he, too, was like those children
and so were his friends
and so were his entire people
they were like those children,
Destroyed by hatred
Destroyed by evil.
Ibrahim heard a voice within him
shouting at him to do something, to prevent
the hatred from overwhelming him
But at this point even the air he was breathing was
permeated with it
Hatred
At this point even the ground he was treading upon was
contaminated with it
Land of hatred.

* * *

"God, Ahmed, you always have a book in your hands! I don't understand how you can keep from being bored . . ."

"Being bored? Are you joking? Reading is like getting aboard a train that's taking you, you don't now where. And when you have to get off, you feel so sad . . ."

"For me you're not completely normal. What book is it, anyways?"

"*Hamlet.* Shakespeare. I have read it a thousand times, but each time the pages draw me in and I can't break away until I have finished it. The main character has incredible charm, and the cunning of a fox . . . I mean, I think people underestimate those who might seem mentally unstable, and Hamlet, pretending to be crazy, succeeds in avenging the murder of his father. And then his troubled love with Ophelia . . . until the end we wonder if the beautiful young girl has really conquered the heart of such a restless boy . . ."

"I can see that books are making you become a bit silly, Ahmed. Why don't we play a good round of chess, instead? We'll form two teams, then . . ."

"Ibrahim, you guys go ahead, I have to finish the book. Sorry."

"You're completely crazy."

*   *   *

The morning of March 12, 1998, Ibrahim was leaving to go to work,
Mohammad and Ramy were with him, they had to go to the hospital,
they were walking along, chatting,
suddenly Ibrahim stopped
at the end of the little street that led to their house he saw a male figure
he called to his friends, look, someone is coming,
he seems to be coming toward us
he looked like a young man
Ibrahim felt his heart skip a beat as, standing still, he watched the man draw near
Ramy and Mohammad also seemed stopped by a strange force that was holding their feet nailed to the ground

The man was now a few meters away
He had a beard, straight light chestnut hair
large, really large brown eyes
he was looking at them
the commotion, the tears
the amazement,
the intensity of overwhelming feelings
one after another
sometimes you have the feeling that what is happening
has already happened many times and that you are in
some way repeating it for the nth time
but the truth is that it has happened in our heads, in our
dreams,
in our desires,
Ibrahim had dreamed that moment so often
he had wanted it so much
it was happening
it was happening
but now no one was able to move,
Mohammad let go a strange suffocated gasp,
Ramy's eyes were open wide,
Ibrahim felt a violent wave assaulting his heart, his mind
was it happiness?
Was it surprise?
Allahu akbar
and he saw a man who was staring at him
he was a very tall, thin man
with a lean, angular face, thin lips, aquiline nose
and very large eyes, which seemed not to go
with all the rest of his face
he had the air of a gentle and cordial man
and he continued to stare at Ibrahim, but not with

hostility or suspicion
but rather with kindness,
and he saw a man who was staring at him
and he saw a man who was staring at him
Ibrahim remembered that other moment, five years
before, but so clear in his mind
so clear
Ibrahim remembered that moment and felt tears
threatening to gush forth,
he saw a boy with a lean, angular face
and he saw an Ibrahim still beardless
he saw two youths
with such uncertainties in their lives
he saw the beginning of it all,
he saw an almost sacred friendship,
he saw the promise of three years before,
"and we will fight . . . we will fight to the death."
"They had promised to never leave each other
Never leave each other
They had promised to fight to the death
And neither would ever abandon the other
Nedal had broken the promise
But now he had returned.

As soon as Ibrahim was able to move, he exploded into a
    cry and hurled himself upon his
    friend,
    they both fell to the ground, laughing and crying,
    they got back up, hugged each other almost to the point
    of pain,
    fell down once again, got back up,
    laughed, sobbed, embraced,

the emotion, Ibrahim was trembling
Nedal couldn't see a thing,
his eyes were so blinded by tears,
when they had the strength to break away
and to look at each other
it seemed as if they were sniffing each other out, like a
pup and its mother that have found each other again
Nedal had a beard, he was even thinner,
he had another expression,
more aware,
more mature,
Ibrahim's face was turned and
What struck Nedal
What shook him
What wounded him
Was to see that the light,
The light that Ibrahim had had in his eyes
for so long
had disappeared, or maybe it had grown dim
His face emanated a certain air of resignation,
of becalmed suffering,
of melancholy impotence
Ibrahim had lost something during those years
While they were observing each other,
Mohammad shouted, realizing
who was there,
he flung himself upon Nedal,
and he embraced him, kissed him,
then it was Ramy's turn
Riham, hearing the excited voices and the emotional
shouts,
came out of the house

but she froze at the threshold
she felt her head spinning,
she staggered, immediately recovered her balance, she
leaned against the doorjamb
her eyes looking into his eyes,
while Mohammad, Ramy, Ibrahim
watched them, immobile
a magical moment
a glance full of words, feelings
throats dry, temples throbbing furiously,
a hammering in the heart,
Riham's sweet face
crossed by one, two tears
her hand to her mouth,
a smothered cry
Nedal holds back his tears, doesn't dare move,
his heart cries out
his heart cries,
he feels a pain in his heart
he looks at her,
she is so beautiful
so beautiful
he didn't remember that she was so beautiful
her long hair, smooth as silk,
her gray eyes, intense, deep
Nedal's glance drowns them,
drowns them,
and it is a sweet oblivion
a sweet, painful oblivion
they stay there discovering each other, looking at each
other for a moment
which seems an eternity

it is as if time had stopped
as if it had stopped,
then a shout, it seems the heart cannot support
an emotion so intense,
a happiness so complete,
while the pain and euphoria merge,
while they embrace, hug each other, sum up
in a single gesture
the hardship and the sorrows and the suffering
and the melancholy and the nostalgia
of two years,
while it seems that love rules over every other feeling,
while the exhaustion of such an intense moment seems
to destroy the fragility
of a woman in love
of a woman who has dreamed, cried, desired
her man,
who had to put aside her feelings and
forget that love was a sentiment
so strong,
it takes your breath away,
it stops your heartbeat,
it saps your energy,
a woman who seemed to have forgotten
that anything so intense might exist
within her
tears, tears, pain,
happiness, emotion
Then Gihad and Ahmed came out
they saw Nedal
Gihad lurched
toward Nedal,

hugged him hard, laughed, hugged him, laughed
Ahmed stayed to the side
he didn't know who this tall, thin man was
with his lean, angular face, his large eyes
but he had to be someone very important,
they were all crying,
they all seemed like prisoners of some new feeling,
unusual,
they seemed overwhelmed by an extremely strong
emotion,
Ahmed didn't know who this man was
but he understood that he had to be a person
who was very important.

Many months must have passed because they had all
become used to Nedal's presence.
In the morning they awoke and sought him out with
their eyes, to be sure that it all was true,
That it hadn't been a dream
And that their friend Nedal was with them once again
Riham never left his side, and then he spoke only to her,
Gihad and Ahmed spent all day teasing them,
Mohammad and Ramy were calm and seemed to be
infected with Ahmed's sarcasm and irony,
Ibrahim felt a strong sense of protection for them
and he was happy to see them all so united and cheerful
like a father might be when he sees that his own children
are healthy and happy
The war had now passed onto a second level, they were
all trying to not see, or rather to pretend to not see the
soldiers and tanks and weapons, what mattered was that
they were all together,

Ibrahim and Mohammad built some new beds,
At this point their family had become large
On April 21, 1999, Riham and Nedal were married,
it was an extremely happy day and they celebrated until
the following day,
Mohammad gave his room, the largest one, to the two
newlyweds,
they cleaned it until it shone and they decorated it with
flowers,
they bought a double bed, a dressing table,
Mohammad set up a bed for himself in Ramy's and
Ibrahim's room,
while Ahmed and Gihad slept in a little room with walls
covered with verses from the Qur'an.
Nedal found work at a car dealership, Ahmed with a
mechanic, Gihad in a restaurant
Life continued,
and the last member of their family, the youngest,
arrived in September,
they found him on the street, laughing as he begged,
laughing as he begged,
he was all dirty, he had two broken teeth, his hair
uncombed, the air of a clown, his name was Ualid,
he was only thirteen, very young,
he had been begging since he was seven, he had spent
half his life on the street, but finally he had found a family,
one he had never had,
his name was Ualid,
he was thirteen.

PART THREE

IT IS A COLD NIGHT, A FULL MOON, THE STARS INFINITE,
they seem like freckles on a face,
Ibrahim takes a puff on a cigarette
he thinks, he is remembering, it is a strange evening,
nostalgia seems to be taking the upper hand
nostalgia is overruling everything
He remembers many things, beginning with his mother,
he doesn't remember what her face was like, and he
doesn't have even a photograph, his father was his only
tie to the past and thus to his mother, he saw a photograph only once, from their wedding
She was very beautiful
Very beautiful
Ibrahim is remembering his father's face,
that one he remembers well
he sees it every night,
then that day, the blood, the Qur'an, it is all very clear in
his memory,
he doesn't understand if it's a blessing or a curse,
his meeting up with Nedal, with Gihad and Riham,
then Mohammad and Ramy,

Ahmed
Nedal's return
And finally Ualid
The quiet of the night is broken by the booms
of Kalashnikovs,
the usual incursions of Israeli soldiers into nearby villages,
the army moves in with heavy artillery
It seems incredible
incredible
that a few kilometers from home
hatred and violence can be raging,
that there is war
so close to where you sit drinking some tea
with your friends
Ahmed comes out on the balcony, he smiles seeing
Ibrahim's absent look, almost lost in space
he tells him,
"I have always wondered, really, what you're thinking
when you're so distant"
Ibrahim rouses himself from his thoughts, barely smiles
and answers:
"About so many things. I'm thinking of so many things.
I'm thinking that our Intifada has now lasted over a year but
the only thing we have gained is a terrifying number of
dead. I'm thinking about September thirtieth of last year,
when that child, Mohamed Aldorra, was killed and when
they interviewed the soldier who had killed the boy he said
he had let the father live in order to make him suffer, that's
what. The fact that that soldier said something like that
seems to upset me alone. The rest of the world could care
less. People are of the opinion that this is only one of so
many small victims, that's what. And now I'm thinking, does

public opinion still matter? Well, I think absolutely not," Ibrahim says with a bitter smile. "I wonder what the rest of the world is thinking. What will they show young people in the West on TV? What do they think about what is happening? Are they interested in the fact that people are dying here? That's what I was thinking about," Ibrahim says, "among other things," then he grows silent, takes another puff, looks into the darkness of the night, tries to give a smile, turns toward Ahmed, says to him:

"And what are you thinking about?"

And Ahmed looks at him, also smiles, and his eyes grow bright:

"I was thinking that I could stay here reading until the end of the world. But in the end the only thing that matters to me are all of you. And you. I was thinking that you have given me a family, that you are my family, and that maybe I never say it to you enough, that I truly love you, and well then, maybe one day we will no longer be close and I won't be able to tell you. Thank you thank you for everything you have done for me. If this war should end some day and we could have our land, if some day we get beyond all this violence, then, I would like to be able to be close to you and ask you, Have you seen what we have done, what we have done?"

Ahmed stays silent, he looks at his hands, maybe embarrassed

When you are a man it is difficult for you

Difficult

to let yourself go and admit that your heart is burning

with a feeling so delicate that it beyond all suffering, and

it is love

It is love

They look at each other
Ibrahim remembers the first time he made him a
promise, the first time he had lied to him
It was about Ashgan, he had told him
she will make it, Ahmed, she will make it
and now he doesn't want to promise Ahmed that one
day they both will be here and they will be close
because he knows that it might not be true
but he limits himself to smiling at him again
and lowering his glance
Ibrahim feels he has aged so much
it's absurd because in reality he is only thirty-one,
the devil, he feels a rage growing within him if he thinks
about it, he is only thirty-one years old and he should be
tasting the good things life has to offer and smiling more
often,
instead he is living with seven friends and he is afraid
for them every day, every day, and every evening he
goes out on the balcony and looks at the sky, the moon,
the heavens, he marvels that this day too has passed,
without anything happening to any of the people he
loves, Ibrahim thinks back to that girl he had met a few
years earlier, that Yasmin, who was speaking of peace
with such conviction,
he would like it if people, all people of the world
would think like Yasmin
so very many victims would be spared
a boom rips through the night
and reminds Ibrahim that it is too late for these thoughts.

"Ramy, stop it, for God's sake, can't you lend a hand instead
of always arguing with Gihad?"

"Listen, Riham, if your brother continues to provoke me, how can I react?"

"Go call Ibrahim and Ahmed, instead they should be on the balcony! Then pay attention to the water, see if it's boiling . . ."

"I know how to make tea, Riham!"

"All right, all right, I'm going out with the garbage."

"Ibrahim, Ahmed! Riham says to come in!"

"Ok, we're coming in, just a second!"

"GIHAD! Stop acting like a fool! Bring me the tea, instead."

"Why don't you get it, Mohammad? What, am I your servant?"

"Gihad, I'm not in the mood for this! If you make me angry . . ."

"If I make you angry what? What will you do, huh? Hit me? Slap me around? And then? I'll call my sister and she'll give you a good . . . aaaaah! Stay away from me! Oooouf! You're so heavy! Get off me . . . no! Don't tickle me, no! Rihaaaaam! Aaaaah . . . get off, Mohamm . . . aaah ah, no I beg you! Don't tickle me! Get off!"

"Hey, you two what are you up to?"

"He's the one who started it, Riham! He jumped on top of me with all his kilos of fat!"

"Fat? Me? I'm all muscle, you idiot!'

"Hey, is this some sort of battlefield? And you, Mohammad, what are you doing there on top of Gihad?"

"Oh, nothing, Ibrahim . . . we were . . . talking . . ."

"Excuse me, but you have to stay on top of him to talk?"

"You, Ahmed, mind your own business!"

"The tea, Love? Hey . . . but what are you two doing?"

"Well, Nedal was the only one missing. All right, we will settle up another time. Instead, Riham, serve the tea."

"All right, all right, I'm bringing it. I'm coming right away."

"Boys, this is an extraordinary gathering! Everyone seated!"

"Well, you fool, get up, I was first!"

"Listen, Gihad, if you don't get up I am telling Mohammad to finish things off . . . "

"No, no, Mohammad no! Come on, Ramy, sit down on the sofa. I'm settled in here."

"Okay, here's the tea. Take it, darling. Ibrahim . . . this one with two sugars is for Ahmed. Ualid, this is yours. Gihad, stop being a jerk with Ramy. Mohammad, this is for you, pass the other one to Ramy. And this one is for me. There."

"Well then, now that each of you has his own tea, may I begin the meeting?"

"Meeting? What meeting?"

"Pssst, Riham! Ibrahim has called a special meeting . . . "

"Precisely. A special meeting. So, guys, I'll get to the point immediately: this month our accounts don't balance. We paid the rent and the bill at the market, and also the water bill. But if we don't pay the electricity bill, they'll cut it off. Unfortunately, I have already collected my wages and we paid the rent, and so I have to ask you to give me all the money you have, otherwise we'll soon be without lights."

"Well, it's not that it changes much if we pay! We paid for the water, but there isn't any today anyway and we had to go to the well to get some! At this point, whether we pay the bills or not, sooner or later we'll be without lights anyway!"

"I agree with Gihad, Ibrahim, after all, maybe we shouldn't pay . . . "

"But what are you saying, Mohammad? We need electricity, we can't risk having them cut it off!"

"But yes, come on, guys, Ibrahim is right, we need electricity. So take out your money."

"Oh, okay, I'll give what I have left from my wages. Anyway, at the dealership who knows what they'll pay me."

"Tomorrow they should pay me, at the garage. I'll bring you half my wages."

"Fine, I see that we are in agreement. Thank you, Nedal, and thank you, Ahmed. Now, the second topic is Ualid. He needs to go to school, it's wrong for him to not even have an elementary school diploma."

"Hey, I don't want to go to school! I'm fine like this!"

"Ualid, now you're acting like a baby! You have to have a minimum of instruction, you have to learn mathematics and geography and history, and all the other subjects. We have all gone at least through middle school; education is indispensable for everyone. So we need to send you to school. At this point we have decided; it's only a question of where."

"But I don't want to go there, to school! I have lived my entire life on the street. Why do I have to bother with school?"

"To learn! And don't make a scene!"

"Listen Ibrahim, I have an idea. I think that you cannot send him to school without a minimum knowledge of the basics, and so, since I'm the only one here not working, and I'm only sewing socks and preparing meals and tidying up the rooms, I can give him some lessons, which might last even six, seven hours a day. We'll buy some books, and I will teach him a bit. Then next year we'll enroll him in middle school! After all, Ualid doesn't even know how to read and write."

"Riham is right, Ibrahim. You can't send an illiterate to middle school. And this way she would have something to do, instead of sewing socks, as she says. I, in any case, have never given you socks to sew."

"Right, you leave them with their holes in the closet, my dear! I'm the one who takes them out and fixes them! Anyway what do you think, Ibrahim?"

"Well . . . yes, maybe you're right. All right, let's give him a break for a year."

"No, no and no again! I am not going to school not even in a hundred years! And I'm not taking lessons from Riham the crazy one!"

"What did you call me? You wretch!"

"Calm down, Riham. He's a little boy, he's only joking. Listen, where does this hatred for school come from?"

"I don't want to waste my time listening to a dumb teacher! I want to kill soldiers, throw stones at them and harass them as much as I can. I want to kill them all and . . . "

"UALID! What are you saying? What sort of ideas are these? I'll kill you! You stupid fool! Come here, as my name is Ibrahim, I'm going to kill you! WRETCH!"

"Well, Calm down Ibrahim! Stop it, what are you doing? What is this outburst? I have never seen you so angry!"

"Nedal, do you hear how he's talking? Like an assassin! He doesn't give a damn about learning things, no sir, nooo, he only wants to kill soldiers! Have you understood this little boy? I will get these ideas out of his head! Listen carefully, Ualid. I want peace in this house. I also want to win. And we know that to win you sometimes need to play tough, and often you need to do to the enemy what the enemy does to you. But this is not your job. You just have to study, to grow. You have to pray to Allah. It isn't your job to throw stones and kill soldiers! Get these ideas out of your head!"

"But if my father were alive, he would be doing this! All the boys on the street are throwing stones!"

"Maybe those boys don't have parents. You instead do, we are all your parents. And we don't want you to do things like this. So starting tomorrow you will take lessons from Riham. I don't want to discuss it further."
Ibrahim felt his anger still burning inside him,
he got up, went out on the balcony again
while his friends stayed without moving, in the living room, dismayed
Ibrahim had a violent reaction
If Nedal hadn't stopped him, he probably would have thrown a punch at Ualid, and this amazed them because Ibrahim was always good and kind with everyone, especially the boy
Ibrahim is nervous, irritated
He can't stand seeing a young boy of fifteen
and moreover a young boy for whom he is responsible
who wants to dedicate his life to killing people
Ibrahim holds his head in his hands, stays still for a few minutes,
Then goes back inside and apologizes to his companions,
he turns and goes to lie down and sleep

"Ibrahim! Ibrahim!"
"Mmm?"
"Are you awake?"
"Yes . . . that is, now yes . . . what is it, Nedal?"
"I'd like to speak to you, Ibrahim."
"At three in the morning?"
"Would you rather we talk tomorrow?"
"Very well, at this point. Wait for me to put something on. Wait for me outside . . ."
"All right."

"This is crazy. To wake me at three in the morning to talk . . . "

"Are you there?"

"Yes, Nedal, I'm coming . . . uff . . . here, I'm coming . . . here I am. And so?"

"Sit down."

"All right. Tell me."

"Here, it's about Riham and me. You know that we have been married for two years. . . and . . . well, for two years we have been trying to have children."

"Yes, certainly. And so?"

"Yesterday we went to the gynecologist, Ibrahim, do you know that for some time now she has been nauseous and constantly dizzy?"

"Yes, so?"

"You still don't understand, do you?"

"No, what does the gynecologist have to do with it?"

"You're really thick! Ibrahim, Riham is two months pregnant."

"What? Pregnant? But . . . pregnant, are you sure? Allah be praised! This really is news! Wow! Nedal, but this is great! Aaah, what fun! Nedal a father! God, I can't imagine it! And why didn't you tell everyone, this evening?"

"It was really hard for Riham. I don't know, I wanted you to know a bit before the others. Well, it's wonderful news . . . "

"Certainly! So is it a boy or a girl?"

"Ibrahim, it's only the second month! You can't know that yet!"

"Good God. Nedal is finally becoming a father! Isn't it absurd? Hey, you who said you would never take the plunge! I can't imagine how happy Riham must be!"

"Really, she keeps talking about all the things we need to buy for the baby and she already has started to knit away. The only thing is . . . here . . . in precarious times like these, I wonder if it is right to have a child. We . . . I know, it is sad, it's awful to say this, but Riham and I could very well not be here tomorrow, we cannot assure our child a stable, calm future. Do we have the right to bring into the world a baby who will grow up to be a copy of Ualid, full of bitterness, hatred, violence? Do we have the right?"

"I understand what you're saying, Nedal. But we have to escape from it, from this war, and the only way to do this is to try to live a normal life and to surround ourselves with normal gestures, facts, moments. You want a child, Nedal, and now I'm telling you that it is your right to have one. But then it will be your duty to educate it with solid principles, and if you don't want him to become a clone of all the other wild children, then teach him the way of God and direct his mind toward a peaceful and faithful path. Don't surrender to the war. This is so wonderful, Nedal. Believe me, this is spectacular news! I just can't wait for the others to know!"

"I . . . thank you, Ibrahim. I think that you're right. I want to thank you, Ibrahim, we have known each other for eight years and you have been my friend for eight years, without reservation, you have never betrayed me."

"Oh, stop it. You're making me cry now."

"No, really, You have never asked me what I did during the two years I spent away from you. And I wanted to keep it to myself. Here then, during those two years I tried to pull away from a bond that seemed too profound, too real. It was my way of surrendering to the war. But I came out of it when I returned to all of you, and now I don't want to make the same mistake again. I really love you, Ibrahim. You are everything to me. I lost my mother, my sister. My father has not returned from Syria, I don't even know if he is still alive. And now I am rebuilding a life for myself, and you are the pillar on which I am resting. I really love you."

"I too, Nedal. However things turn out, our friendship is eternal."

* * *

"Ibrahim! Ibrahim! Wake up, hurry up, come on! IBRAHIIM!"

"Aaaaaah . . . what . . . ?"

"Ibrahim, WAKE UP!"

"Aaah . . . stop it, idiot! Get out!"

"It's an emergency! You dope, wake up! Soldiers, hurry up!"

"Soldiers? What? Which ones?"

"Wake up, Ibrahim!"

"Bu . . . Nedal . . . what's happening?"

"Israeli soldiers! Seven hundred, eight hundred meters away! There must be about ten! There's a brawl, Ualid provoked them! Get up!"

It's no use, Ibrahim is already up, flying toward the room where Ahmed, Mohammad, and Ramy sleep, flying toward Ahmed's backpack, unzips it—it's no use, he knew it—nothing, the pistol isn't there, he runs toward the door, he trips, falls, bangs his knee violently, but he gets up, gets up, runs, runs, hears Nedal's breath close by, then he turns for a moment, looks at Nedal: "Your wife, where is your wife?" but Nedal nods, as if to tell him she is safe, don't worry, they run, finally they get there, they see, shots, cries, overturned cars protect the boys and the men, soldiers with machine guns in hand, from across the street, they are shooting somewhat at

random, and you see deliberate shots, a stone strikes a
soldier in the head, the soldier falls, his companion
drags him to the side and fires toward the man who
threw the stone, he hits him, grazing his arm, the man
collapses, he picks up another stone and throws it with
his right arm, then he hides behind a Fiat, Ibrahim sees
Ualid on the ground, Mohammad, Ramy, and Gihad
around him, is it serious? Serious? no, no it mustn't be
serious, it can't be, he's not breathing, you run, it's
important, you run, there, a lot of blood, confusion, they
are screaming, Ualid on the ground, on the ground,
blood, blood, his dry lips are moving—what? what?—
can you tell me what's happening, and you hear a word,
only one word, in the uproar and in the clamor of the
battle you distinctly hear that little word

mama

and the war continues,
God,
Careful, no, cover him, hurry, take him inside,
Mohammad strikes a soldier, he falls, falls, gets back up,
he fires into thin air, Ramy hurls another stone at him,
strikes him in the eye, he lifts his hand to his eye and
Gihad hurls a stone, hits him in the head, he falls, falls
but doesn't get up again, then they hear a shot, a shot, it
is a machine gun, a scream, Ramy falls to the ground, no!
nooo, someone cries, it is Ibrahim, Ibrahim, for God's
sake, it is Ibrahim, careful
Ramy's leg, if he holds it up, is full of blood, it's nothing,
nothing, only his leg,
only his leg?

If it becomes gangrene . . . Stupid, call an ambulance,
God, an ambulance, Mohammad has a cell phone, he
carries Ualid and Ramy to the house—who knows
how—and calls the ambulance, he calls it, hurriedly,
hurry up, I beg of you, it's serious, many wounded,
Nedal goes quickly, he hurls stones, hurls, hurls, in
a hurry, rapid movements, certain, balanced, he has a
strong arm, a lot of power, two, two soldiers, he takes out
two, he's lucky, the machine gun strikes him only grazing
him, his hand, but he is fortunate because they aim at
him many times but don't strike him, stones, again
A strong arm
Ibrahim isn't even aware of the constant, rapid, almost
mechanical movement, gather, aim throw
Gather, aim, throw
throw
gather
throw
throw
throw
they are afraid, all of them, pure adrenaline, you need to
be swift, swift
kill before they kill you
it's dangerous,
fear,
throw,
Ibrahim realizes that he has taken down four or five, not
bad, not bad,
the problem is that then they get back up
God, pray to God
bism Allah al rahmen al rahim, In the name of thy Lord
who created, thy Lord is the most

Noble,

fear.

but where is Ahmed, where is he? And then there he is,
you spot him, he is there, but something is happening, he
turns the car, his shelter, he settles himself twenty
meters away from them, or less, and he shoots, he
shoots, four shots come out, four soldiers four, and while
he is about to take the fifth, about to, that's it about to
shoot, his eye nervous, is it a tic?—since when does
Ahmed have a tic?—lips closed tight, eye bright, hand
still, still?, no, it's trembling, it's trembling—it seems
absurd but everyone, for a moment, stops fighting and
notices a hand that is trembling—
a hand that's trembling
it's trembling
trembling
shaken by small movements that follow rapidly one after
another
moved by small oscillations
jolted from within
the hand, the eye
trembles,
the shot is fired, fired, no, it's not one shot, there are two,
how can it be? How can it be? A single pistol, a single
instant, two shots? How is it possible, no, it is not scien-
tifically possible, there is something that doesn't make
sense, no, because there isn't one pistol, there are two,
or rather a pistol and a rifle,
a pistol stolen from a dead Israeli soldier
and a MADE IN USA rifle, received a month before, by an
Israeli soldier,
twenty-eight years old, Jon Königsberg, perfect aim,

special ability
he's a good shot
good
before going into the service he didn't even know how
to knock down the little ducks at the amusement park
now he has a perfect aim,
he shoots, two shots are heard, one into thin air, thin air,
which one? Ahmed's
the other hits the mark, the mark, which? The one
meant for Ahmed
for Ahmed
the carotid artery
funny, because later the doctor will say that the bullet
hit right on the carotid, it pierced it,
it passed through to the other side
a perfect shot
Ahmed has fallen, Ahmed falls, his light body, the body
of a dreamer, of a thinker, of one who likes to read—a
lot—of one who was reading—always—he was twenty-
three, Ahmed, he was the youngest after Ualid, he had
many dreams—he wanted to write a book, to travel, to
marry and have many children, to win, to win, and to
live in peace in HIS land, he only wanted to live, he
didn't want his Palestinian homeland to conquer the
world, nor for the Palestinian State to expand its
territories, he only wanted a Palestinian State, but all he
got was a bullet to the carotid artery, twenty-three
birthdays, the last four passed in silence, it is the war,
damnation, the war, Ahmed falls.

Madness, delirium, Ibrahim a protagonist in a tragedy
    that Ahmed would have called Shakespearean,

Hamlet, who raves, who flees, who yells,
the red that penetrates the skin,
into the soul
and lashes out.
He read, Ahmed,
and if Ibrahim, too, had read that *Hamlet,*
maybe he would have known
that one doesn't reemerge
from madness

Moments in which it is difficult to understand, difficult
    because—in which maybe, if
    only, you might disappear, disappear, because the feel-
    ings, the emotions, are too strong—strong—and maybe
    you can't sustain it, damnation, damnation, photos,
    memories, something, objects, objects, not people,
    people, you venture for a hand, a grasp, an embrace,
    the person, not objects—he was only twenty-three—
    and his parents? Where might his parents be? Why?
    Does he have parents, then? Ahmed had been with them
    since he was five, five, and he had never —never—spo-
    ken about his family, but did it exist, then, a family?
    Damnation, it's not right, if there were a family, for them
    not to be informed, a mother, a father, shouldn't they
    know about it? It would be right, but they don't know
    anything about Ahmed, except his age and name, and
    that he liked to read, a family? A past?, no thank you, it
    meant nothing in that house, it was enough to have the
    desire to win, to fight, to be young and brave, they all
    loved each other, they knew each other, but they asked
    nothing about the past, no, because each was what he
    was, neither past nor future were of any interest, only

the present, and despite, despite this they all knew each
other so well and they each trusted in the other, in
extraordinary fashion—why?—and yet no answer
exists, maybe, God, maybe, if Ibrahim had woken up
first? But why so late, why in that way, why, you don't
know, you don't understand—God, he was only fifteen
years old—now he wished he had never given him those
two slaps, and he also would have let him smoke, what
was it, after all, what was a bit of nicotine? Nothing, if
you think that now he is no longer here, he isn't here,
Riham? where is Riham? blood, truth, why? no, her heart
will no longer hold out, Riham is on the ground, why?
why? why did you leave her alone? God, she was
pregnant, pregnant, one life, two lives, oh well, that's
how it is, like that, Riham is dead—dead?—she's no
longer alive, no longer? Ualid is dead—dead?—he's no
longer alive, fifteen years old, there are so many things
Ualid has never done, and he will never do, Ahmed,
Ahmed, brave, God, he was so brave, dead, dead, they
have amputated Ramy's leg—no, I beg you, nooo, leave
my leg, I beg you, my leg, *allahu akbar*, I beg you—tears,
like those of a child, those of a child, God, they amputated it, Ramy is in the hospital, God, why, a breath of
cold air, air, dries the tears, dries them, dries them up,
why? God, help me to suffer
help me to suffer,
let these tears flow
Ibrahim is dead, dead, he is no longer alive, or, if he
does live, he lives in another dimension
a dimension of death, sorrow
but is he still alive? If he wonders, if he wonders—am I
still alive?—a tear, two, a thin moon,

thin as the thread that separates life from death,
a sky full of stars—full—luminous points that frame the
elegant vault of the night,
and tears—tears—copious, infinite, Ibrahim thinks
thinks
he still has a life of tears
he could cry until he dies
dies
It no longer matters
he hates
he hates
don't ask what, he hates, at this moment, he hates death
and he hates love
the love that now makes him suffer
he hates the soldiers
he hates any Israeli that lives on the face of the earth
it is an unconditional, irrational hatred that you cannot
explain, justify
but also not criticize
no
no you can't, tears
again,
he prays to God, he prays to God, one day all this will
end—it will end—but
Ibrahim will no longer be there.

Ramy saw the amputation of his own leg with hatred and
    grief
    and he gulped down a small bottle of medicine
    Mohammad stopped working at the hospital
    and devoted his life
    to prayer

he lost all touch with reality and ended up going mad
they put him away in a psychiatric ward
Nedal hated every day that he remained alive without
his wife
and the small life he had created together with her
until he got involved in a shootout and was killed by two
soldiers
Gihad left Palestine and went to Syria where he sought
in vain to rebuild a life
Now he wanders unfeeling and unaware
He lives because Allah wishes it
Ibrahim
Ibrahim dies every day along with a Palestinian
companion,
a baby,
a woman,
a man,
along with the Intifada and those who are fighting it.

I dedicate this story, in which the characters and events (except some news items) are exclusively the product of my imagination, to Mohamed Gamal Aldorra, twelve years old, dead like Ahmed, like Ualid, without reason, with courage, I dedicate this story to him and I pray for him because wherever he is now, wherever he might be, he has something better than the hatred and death of this war.

— RANDA GHAZY